The Coldest Day In Texas

The Coldest Day in Texas

Peggy Purser Freeman

A Chaparral Book for Young Readers

Texas Christian University Press
Fort Worth

Copyright © 1996 by Peggy Purser Freeman

Library of Congress Cataloging-in-Publication Data

Freeman, Peggy (Peggy P.)
   The coldest day in Texas / by Peggy Freeman
      p.   cm. — (A Chaparral book)
   Summary: In 1899, as prairie fires rage through the Texas Panhandle, twelve-year-old Shyanne struggles with her guilt over the death of her twin sister Shenandoah in a blizzard the previous winter and her crush on the most popular boy in class.

   ISBN 0-87565-169-0 (alk. paper)
   [1. Texas—Fiction. 2. Fires—Fiction. 3. Blizzards—Fiction. 4. Death—Fiction. 5. Twins—Fiction. 6. Sisters—Fiction 7. Fires—Fiction] I. Title.

PZ7.F876Ca   1997
[Fic]—dc20   96-26823
                                   CIP
                                   AC

Design by Margie Adkins
Cover painting by Don Punchatz

DEDICATION

In memory of my sister, Ouida Purser Eiland, who led me to the altar of the First Methodist Church in Tulia, where we found unconditional love; to our mom, Sylvia Elam Purser, who taught us to hope; and to the people of Swisher County, who gave us the courage to follow our dreams.

ACKNOWLEDGEMENTS

Special thanks to the editors of *Windmilling*, a history of Swisher County, for their labor in preserving county history. Thanks to all my critique partners, my sister, Ruth Sims, and other friends who have shared their knowledge so willingly. Last and most important, thanks to my husband, Dickey, and my best friends—my daughters, Stephanie Nance and Cynthia Freeman.

Chapter One

The coldest day in Texas was also the day I found out I was in love with Josh Paul Younger, just like every other sappy, twelve-year-old girl who lived in Swisher County in the Texas Panhandle. And it was the day I lost my best friend, my twin sister, Shenandoah Jones. The Texas Almanac recorded February 12, 1899, as the coldest day in Texas history.

It was Josh Paul's favorite saying, "The coldest day in Texas." He would ride up to the school, slide off Feller's back and say, "That horse is meaner than the coldest day in Texas." Later, you could hear him mumbling as he left school, "This has been the worst day, worse than the coldest day in Texas." In the summertime, Josh Paul just changed cold to hot and started all over.

A week before Valentine's Day, I felt like I was coming down with the croup. Shenandoah had had it the week before, but she caught everything. Doc Anderson said she suffered with a condition—a weak heart formed when she and I were still in Mama's stomach.

I knew I had to be coming down with some kind of sickness. That morning, when I accidentally touched Josh Paul's hand as we watered the teacher's little pine tree planted next to the school, my knees felt all weak and funny. Furthermore, at lunch time, I sat down on the bench by him and Shenandoah, and I couldn't swallow a bite of my bacon-and-biscuit-soaked-in-molasses sandwich.

"The croup," I assured myself. Our brothers, Augusta, Jackson, Murfrees, Russell and Shawnee had coughed for a week. Each of us were named after a place Mama and Papa had lived.

1

Like a map, our names stretched from Virginia to Texas.

Right after lunch, in the middle of geography, I looked at Josh Paul and he, of course, was staring at my sister. Shenandoah was the most beautiful girl in Swisher County. Her blond hair curled down her back in natural ringlets, while mine could be rolled in rags for a month of Sundays and not have one wave. Even her name sounded as if it came out of a fancy magazine. Mine, Shiloh Anne, was disgusting! Mama said if people talked to me when I was little, I'd hide behind Shenandoah and blush. I got stuck with Shyanne for a nickname. Completely disgusting!

Shenandoah looked at Josh Paul and smiled her sweetest smile, as wide and pure as the panhandle's horizon.

I leaned my chin on my hands and glanced down at my skinny arms. My hair, not blond and not brown, but a muddy mixture of both, drooped down on my shoulders and fell to the desk before me.

My sister was nice. Mama said I could cause the Archangel himself to spout a stream of cuss words, but not even I could pick a fight with Shenandoah.

Miss Gibson, standing with her back to the window, was talking about something I probably needed to hear, but I knew Shenandoah would remember and repeat it tonight at supper.

"What do you think agriculture is, Shiloh?" Miss Gibson's voice floated by my ears, but her all-knowing look landed right between my hazel eyes.

I thought about the spanking I would get if Papa found out I was daydreaming again. One thing I liked about the Panhandle was the lack of trees. It meant fewer switches. Sometimes Papa made me pick up prairie coal—cow chips, for the fire—instead of spanking me. Picking up prairie coal was worse than a spanking. I moaned my favorite swear word under my breath.

"Oh, cow manure!"

"That's right, Shiloh." Miss Gibson smiled at me.

"Agriculture is using . . . cow manure for fertilizer, rotating crops and breeding better cattle. It's the study of farming and ranching."

Miss Gibson was the best teacher I had ever had. Of course, she was only the third teacher I had ever had. Mama taught Shenandoah and me most of the time.

Miss Gibson touched my shoulder as she passed me on the way to her desk. "Very good, Shiloh," she said softly.

My answer was right? I smiled proudly. I was a genius! I set my mind to Miss Gibson's lesson and thought of how the study of agriculture could make Papa rich.

"My papa says there's not to be any talk of farming around here." Tom Spencer broke into Miss Gibson's discussion on wind-breaks.

"Your father's a rancher, and I understand his concern." Miss Gibson always answered comments like Tom's with patience. I would have tossed him out on one of his big ears just for being rude. Miss Gibson continued gently. "The ranchers are concerned about the free range being bought up and farmed."

"The big ranchers are forgetting they live in a free country." Oscar Roudell spoke up boldly. He was new to Swisher County and didn't know how powerful the ranchers were. "They are putting up so many fences some of us can't get to town."

Several boys started talking at once, each loudly stating his view—or mostly his papa's view—on fences and fence cutting. Miss Gibson tapped her pointer on her desk.

"I guess we need to have a rancher come and give us a lecture on the use of fences." Miss Gibson ended the debate with a third strike of the pointer. Strike four of the pointer would mean no recess. Recess suddenly became more important than each boy's view on the subject. "I'll plan it as soon as possible. Until that time this issue will not be debated on the playground, after school or at Sunday school. Is that clear?" Miss Gibson had been in Texas long enough to know the word "fence" was dangerous.

She continued her lesson on agriculture, and by recess, I had two or three ideas to tell Papa, ideas that could help our herd. Calling Sally and two heifers we hadn't seen much since summer a "herd" was like calling Papa the kind of man that would listen. As I put on my coat and walked out the door, I reminded myself that Papa didn't listen to anyone unless they had a bottle of liquor in their hand and were willing to share it.

I ran out to swing on the hitching rail. Tom Spencer followed me, as usual.

"Lightning struck our windmill last night," he said. Tom Spencer always had a tale of adventure to brag about. No one asked him to tell about it, because we knew he would anyway. "It cracked and zinged louder than the cannon at the parade last summer. The pole lit up and glowed. You couldn't even touch it, it was so hot."

Tom's expressions as he told his wild tale looked like he was in terrible pain. I think that's why we all listened, so we could watch his eyes get big and his mouth twist around like a tornado. The wilder the tale, the wilder his expressions. Josh Paul must have had his fill of Tom's stories, too.

"You're a barnyard bragger, Tom," he said. I had to agree.

"About all I believe of that tale is you have a windmill and it sprinkled last night," I added. Everyone in Tulia had a windmill. It was known as "Windmill City." There was plenty of wind—in Tulia and in Tom's stories. I picked up a hoop and rolled it across the yard. Josh Paul trotted by and yanked my dress sash.

"I'll beat you to the hoop," he cried as he took off.

"You big cheat!" I yelled, running after him.

He gave the hoop another push just before I caught up.

"Rats," I yelled into the north wind. He stopped suddenly and looked at the bank of clouds boiling up in the sky.

"Those look like storm clouds." He squinted his eyes for a better view.

"Do you think it's going to rain?" I asked.

"I think it's going to do worse than that," Josh Paul yelled as he ran inside the school.

Moments later Miss Gibson and Josh Paul stood at the door looking at the sky. The wind whipped through Miss Gibson's auburn hair, pulling wispy curls down around her face. Josh Paul looked more like her son than he did his own mama's. His hair shimmered with the same shade of red.

Uneasy, I darted to where Shenandoah sat on the seesaw. "Josh Paul thinks it's going to storm," I said. It was the first time I had looked at my sister all day. You know how you walk with someone and talk to them, but you don't look at them. Blue tinted her mouth as she shivered.

"Shenandoah Jones," I said, trying to sound like Mama, "you get in that school building, right now." Shenandoah looked up at the windmill towering over us.

"I want to listen to the mockingbird. He barked like a dog this morning," she said. I placed a protective arm around her.

"It wasn't a mockingbird," I insisted. I knew mocking-birds did sometimes bark like a dog, but not in this temperature. "The only thing he would say today is brrr!" I pulled her toward the door. "It's too cold for a mockingbird out here, and it's too cold for you."

"No, it's not. I heard one." She glanced over her shoulder as I pushed her back into the schoolhouse.

Miss Gibson and Josh Paul stood by the window, still talking about the weather. Josh Paul suggested we close school and go home to wait for a snow storm. Everyone got their hopes up except me. I didn't love school, but anything was better than home.

"No, I won't let school out early," Miss Gibson said as she picked up the primer and sat down by the younger students. "You older students read page nine in your reader. Josh Paul, you start." Miss Gibson began reading with the little ones.

Twenty minutes later a knock interrupted our story. Mr. Walsh, who was working on the new church building across the pasture, came blowing in the door with a swirl of snow flakes the size of silver dollars.

"I'd like to pick up my young'uns, Miss Gibson, if you don't mind." Bundled in a heavy coat, a wool scarf and gloves, Mr. Walsh was dressed for the cold weather but still looked frozen. "The temperature is dropping fast. You might better send the kids that live close on home. Josh Paul, you and the Jones girls will never make it out to the creek. You'd better wait here for your folks."

"Do you think it's that bad, Mr. Walsh?" Miss Gibson hadn't spent a winter in Texas and didn't realize the weather could get mean fast.

"It's snowing so hard I could barely see, ma'am." Mr. Walsh buttoned up his kids' coats and wrestled the door open to herd his brood out into the buggy.

"I can't fight all of you and this temperamental weather." Miss Gibson teased. "If you live nearby, go home."

Everybody whooped and hollered. I did too. Miss Gibson wouldn't make us study without the others, and I sure wouldn't miss walking the six miles to our farm.

I grinned at Shenandoah and said, "We'll never get home in time to do our chores."

"I won't get to feed the animals or help Mama with supper," Shenandoah said. She loved doing chores. She had to be either an angel or crazy.

Miss Gibson put away her books and straightened her desk. "Josh Paul, if we're going to wait for a while, you and I better make sure the fire stays warm. Get some more cow chips, please. Shiloh, fix the three of you a snack from my pantry in the coat closet—a third of an apple a piece. Remember your fractions?"

I remembered I couldn't do them. "Yes ma'am," I answered politely. Cutting an apple into equal thirds was as hard as trying to subtract fractions. Fourths I could manage, but I could never tell how to get three pieces of an apple the same size. Josh Paul burst through the door in a gust of frigid air.

"It's bad out," he said. "There ain't nothin' between Texas and the North Pole except a barbed wire fence, and it's down for sure." He turned and added some fuel on the fire. "I doubt my papa can make it in with Feller. That horse is getting mighty old. He's been limping again. That's why I had to walk today."

"I'm sure your father will come," Miss Gibson's smile didn't seem as bright as it did before. "If he doesn't, we'll just make pallets by the fire and stay here tonight." With Miss Gibson, everything was like a picnic. I looked out the window but couldn't see the school's windmill through the blowing snow, much less the town two miles to the southwest. Miss Gibson's eyes followed mine to the storm outside, then rested on my sister.

"Shenandoah, are you warm enough?" Miss Gibson tried to keep the worry from her voice, but it didn't fool me, and I guess it didn't fool Josh Paul.

"It will probably be eighty degrees by tomorrow afternoon." Josh Paul's voice cracked a little. It had been doing that a lot since he turned thirteen.

"Surely, it won't change that fast," Miss Gibson laughed.

"You know what they say about Texas weather." Josh Paul smiled that crooked grin that made my stomach feel queasy. "If you don't like the weather, wait an hour and it will change."

He was right. In an hour the storm changed. It grew worse. Much worse!

Chapter Two

By suppertime the storm sounded like a monster trying to devour the school building. Miss Gibson opened a jar of pickled peaches she had from Bulews' general store. Mrs. Bulew put up peaches she got all the way from East Texas and sold them for a quarter a pint. We said the blessing for the peaches. I remembered to thank God that Mr. Bulew was on the school board and believed in being prepared for one of the many disasters he predicted daily.

As we feasted on saltine crackers and peaches, Shenandoah asked, "Do you think Mama will be worried?"

"Mama won't worry," I said as I slurped the juice off my peach, careful not to miss one drop. "She knows we're with Miss Gibson."

Miss Gibson's brows were drawn together in concern. She didn't realize what a treat this was for Shenandoah and me. The schoolhouse felt warmer than our dugout and was much quieter. But an Indian uprising would be quieter than being in an eight-by-ten-foot room with five brothers under five years old. I was having a grand time.

Josh Paul was determined to ruin my good time. "Hey, Shrimp, you can sure put away a lot of peaches." Josh Paul called me that when he wanted to make me mad. It always worked. Today, his pet name hurt more than usual. I told myself it had to be the croup or a stomach condition.

As the wind howled louder, the cold crept closer to the center of the room. The evening was over too soon. We made pallets out of blankets in the closet, putting them close together and covering ourselves with the heaviest one. Miss Gibson and Shenandoah got in the middle. Josh Paul sprawled out by Miss Gibson and I lay between Shenandoah and the stove. Josh Paul turned on his side and propped himself up on his elbow. The firelight's reflection twinkled in his eyes.

"I never slept on the floor of a schoolhouse. I have slept in the courthouse though. It was in 1890," he said.

I knew a story was coming, but he had called me Shrimp, so I resolved not to listen.

"People started pouring into town like a herd of wild buffalo. All of them telling the same horror stories of Indians butchering the settlers, destroying homes. They were headed straight for Tulia." Josh Paul took off his boots and leaned back against the wall.

"Riders were sent out to warn the settlers, telling them to high-tail it to town and to bring their guns. We dug trenches around the courthouse and the White Hotel," Josh Paul continued his story. By the way his words got low and slowly tripped off his tongue, I knew it would be scary, and I knew I would listen to every word.

"Some men hauled mesquite posts up from Palo Duro Canyon to fortify our stronghold. W.G. Conner took charge, just like he did when he founded Tulia. He sent his best men out at night to guard the town. I was on ground patrol."

"Just what in tarnation is ground patrol?" I asked, thinking to show him up as a braggart for sure.

"We went out of town a ways and placed our ears on the ground to listen for the hoofbeats of horses." Josh Paul's sincerity made me feel like a mean fool. "Listening for a long time makes you jumpy. I expected to hear the blood-curdling war-whoop of the redskins any minute." Josh Paul didn't say anything else.

"Well?" I questioned, irritated with him for making me ask. "What happened?"

"It was a rumor." He laid his head down. "Later we found out that stage driver was jumping to conclusions. He had heard about some Apaches near the New Mexico border and didn't wait to hear about the soldiers with them."

"That's all?" I couldn't believe he wasted a perfectly good Indian story without scaring us a little. "All that trouble, and you didn't even get to see an Indian?"

"Not my fault some old driver liked his whiskey better than the truth. Now if you want to hear about face-to-face meeting up with Indians, that's another story." Josh Paul raised up on his elbow and grinned. "Uncle Pete and I went to Oklahoma the next week to haul supplies for the Tule Ranch. We camped for the night, and I wandered off to shoot a rabbit. About a mile from camp, I heard a clicking sound coming like dozens of butter churns hitting, wood on wood. I crept up the hill, crouching low. A band of Indians was crowded around a field. There had to be twenty lined up in the center like they were ready to do battle."

Now that's more like it, I thought.

"I'd say seventy-five or more natives cheered from the side. I watched from a clump of trees. They started swinging sticks at a small ball. When I crawled closer, I realized they were playing a ball game of sorts. A wild ball game. Turtle shells tied at their knees clicked and clacked as the players ran through the short grass. They tried to hit a leather ball the size of a small apple but usually hit one another instead. Blood splattered every direction. One of the players got hurt. He looked dead." Josh Paul paused for a breath and to let the word "dead" settle in our imaginations.

In the fire's glow I saw him raise his eyebrows and move his eyes like a madman. "Have you ever seen a dead Indian before?"

Shenandoah and I snuggled closer.

"When no one was looking, I crawled up to the makeshift bed where the poor fellow lay and slowly peeped over the edge." Josh Paul's story came out in loud whispers. "The Indian's bloody hand lay limp across his face. I picked up one finger to get a better look at his eyes. Suddenly . . . " Josh Paul grabbed at us.

I jumped and Shenandoah gave a half giggle and a half cough.

"That dead Indian grabbed my arm and wrestled me to the ground."

Shenandoah and I both squealed with delightful fright.

"His eyes looked like he was already on the devil's payroll. He drew a knife and cut . . . the bandage off his other hand. Then he carried me back to the field. Kicking and screaming, I yelled, 'Don't scalp me! Please, don't scalp me.' He and his sidekicks each cackled a big horse-laugh. Then he rushed out to continue the game."

Josh Paul rubbed his freckled nose with the back of his hand and grinned at his own foolishness, then he continued. "After his team won, the Indian put me up on a horse and carried me back to Uncle Pete's camp."

Josh Paul stretched his long frame out on the floor. "I won't be snooping around to look at dead Indians anytime soon."

Even Miss Gibson giggled. I liked Josh Paul's stories, because they were real. Somewhere in the middle of a tale about a jackrabbit and a coyote, I fell asleep.

The short gasp of Shenandoah's breathing woke me up. Mama had trained me to listen for her condition—raspy, short breaths. Tonight she sounded worse than ever.

"Shenandoah, are you all right?" I whispered.

Her answer could barely be heard.

I shook Miss Gibson and she lit the lamp. Shenandoah's hands were an ash-blue color. She struggled to raise her head from the pallet.

Fear showed in Miss Gibson's eyes before she could hide it with a gentle smile. "Why, honey, you should have awakened us sooner," she said as she took Shenandoah in her arms and wrapped a quilt snugly around her.

Josh Paul was up instantly, adding more fuel to the stove and talking about going for the doctor, but I knew that wouldn't help.

"Doc Anderson won't be back in our part of the country until Mrs. Barnes has her baby next month," I said.

"Shiloh's right," Miss Gibson agreed.

"Mama always gives her tea," I offered. "It helps her blood flow faster."

Josh Paul started brewing tea before I could finish the sentence. Miss Gibson covered Shenandoah with the other side of the big quilt.

"We'll just keep you warm, and in the morning your mother and father will drive in and take you home," she said as she cradled Shenandoah in her lap. After she gave her some tea, Miss Gibson sang about the smokey hills of Tennessee. She came from those hills the summer before. Sometimes when she sang about them or watered that little pine tree she had brought from her home, she'd have a glow in her eyes. I knew part of the hills would never leave her. I dreamed of staying in one place long enough for it to feel like home.

🌹 🌹 🌹

When the light woke me the next morning, it wasn't our usual bright sun reflecting on miles and miles of flat snow. The window looked like a sugar bowl, full to the brim. The wind howling across the roof and down the stove pipe gave the room an extra chill. Miss Gibson sat as she had the night before with Shenandoah in her arms. I realized she had sat up all night, and I hadn't stayed awake to help.

"Josh Paul," she asked, sounding worn to a frazzle, "could you go out and get us snow to heat, so we can wash up?"

Josh Paul wasn't good and awake yet. He turned over and grumbled, "Aw, Ma."

Shenandoah slept peacefully, so Miss Gibson lowered her

to the pallet and stood to stretch. I looked at my sleeping sister.

"How is she?" I asked, expecting to hear, "Much better."

Instead Miss Gibson nibbled on her lower lip before she answered. "She's about the same."

I felt I was supposed to know what to do.

"Josh Paul," Miss Gibson called him again as she walked to the washbowl, using the last of the water to splash on her face. "Josh Paul Younger, we need water for tea!" He jumped up with a start and pulled his boots on, then his coat, and grabbed a bucket on the way to the door. The door blew open. Swirling snow demanded all our strength to shut it. The wind and snow drove Josh Paul back, even as he tried to get out.

Concern was written in tiny wrinkles on Miss Gibson's brow. "Wait until the blizzard stops," she said.

"Once it snowed like this for a day and a half," Josh Paul warned her.

"I'm sure it'll stop by noontime," Miss Gibson said, smiling.

It didn't. The wind howled on.

Lunch was sparse. Josh Paul managed to get enough snow in his bucket for tea. We opened a tin of sardines, which I hate. I closed my eyes so that I didn't see them and held my nose so as not to smell them. Shenandoah had only a sip of tea.

After lunch, we were all bored. It occurred to me, music might make Shenandoah feel better, so I asked Miss Gibson to play her mountain dulcimer. "Play the 'Shepherd's Wife's Waltz.' It's my sister's favorite." When Shenandoah barely smiled, my concern grew stronger. Any other time she would waltz and waltz until Mama made her sit down.

The rest of the afternoon we took turns reading and caring for Shenandoah. Miss Gibson and I took stock of the food supplies and counted out how many days we could eat. Josh Paul drew pictures for Shenandoah and told her stories. I couldn't help but feel a little jealous because they were so close. At first, I resented Josh Paul's making Shenandoah laugh so freely. Then I realized it was because I wanted to be laughing with him, not Shenandoah. The thought scared me out of my wits. I didn't like boys. Never did. Never would. And yet there was an ache inside me each time I looked at Josh Paul. And when I looked at him with my sister, the ache turned to a green, sick feeling. My stomach churned with a sour emptiness, like I'd just eaten unripe plums. I was jealous.

Just then Miss Gibson spoke to me. "Josh Paul does have a way with a story, doesn't he?" she asked quietly.

"I don't think they're near as funny as Shenandoah is making them out to be," I said with a bitter tone.

Miss Gibson looked at me carefully.

I should have kept quiet, but I kept talking. "I think she acts like a lovesick calf around him, and he's disgusting when he looks at her."

"Oh, is that it?" Miss Gibson's face didn't smile, but there was a hint of the dimple that comes in her cheek just before she laughs. "Someday, you'll look at someone with that 'sick calf' look."

"No thanks!" I said as I tried to imagine myself with a boyfriend. I could picture me with beautiful hair and a shapely figure. I could see me in a fancy riding outfit, all trimmed in fringed leather, or a low-cut dress like one of the ladies on the front of a dime novel. The problem was that in each image, Josh Paul was the man holding my hand.

I arranged the jars of canned goods on the shelf for the fourth time as though rearranging them would make them multiply. There were still only two jars of pickled peaches left. The rest held beets and turnip greens. I guessed Mr. Bulew's customers didn't like them any more than I did. Miss Gibson's words kept echoing in my head: "Someday you'll look at someone with that sick-calf look."

Each time I looked at Shenandoah and Josh Paul, jealousy grabbed my thoughts, turning them into hateful wishes. I didn't like the way I was feeling but couldn't seem to change it.

Shenandoah hadn't changed. She had always been this beautiful, this sweet. I had always been proud of her. One other fact hadn't changed: compared to her, I was nothing.

By evening I was sick, and it wasn't the croup. I was in love.

"Oh, cow manure!" I whispered.

Chapter Three

Before dark, Josh Paul and Miss Gibson had to go to the shed for more prairie chips to burn. Miss Gibson tied a rope to the doorknob so they could find their way back. I wrestled the door shut and then turned toward Shenandoah.

"Josh Paul would do anything for you, I guess." I didn't look at my sister as I talked.

"He likes to help people, but he's really the one who needs help." Shenandoah leaned up on one elbow. "Josh Paul Younger is tenderhearted and will be hurt often if he doesn't have a wife who looks after him."

If I hadn't been so jealous, I would have seen the pain on her face. "I guess that'll be you." I didn't like the harsh and bitter sounds of my words, but I couldn't stop it.

"No," she answered softly.

"Sure you will, Shenandoah. You're the perfect one. Everybody loves you best. I don't care. I don't want a chance to marry him. Do you hear me?" I raised my voice. "I hate everybody, especially Josh Paul Younger."

"No, you don't hate everyone, and especially not Josh Paul." Shenandoah pulled herself up to her elbow. "You're just growing up and feeling self-conscious."

I hated it when she used grown-up words she had read in some book. "That's right, I just hate you!" As the words flew out of my mouth, I wanted to grab them and stuff them back. Sadness swept over me, a lasting sadness that would be hard to drive away. I had never said anything so mean.

Shenandoah lay back down and closed her eyes.

A torrent of wind and snow blew open the door as Josh Paul and Miss Gibson struggled in with their buckets. They brushed the snow off their coats before it could melt in and soak the material.

After his teeth stopped chattering, Josh Paul said, "It's getting dangerously cold out there."

Miss Gibson set a pan of snow on her desk and then rummaged in the pantry. "I've never seen so much snow in my life," she said as she moved back to her desk and poured sugar and vanilla into the bowl. "That's why I decided to make snow ice cream."

"Wow!" Josh Paul and I both came to see at once. We took turns stirring, our mouths watering with anticipation.

In the midst of the fun of snow ice cream, I noticed how still Shenandoah had become. It was something I felt more than heard, like the time I almost drowned. Shenandoah was helping Mama cook supper and suddenly knew I needed help. They ran to the creek and pulled me up by the bloomers.

I looked at Shenandoah and dropped the spoon to the floor. "Miss Gibson," I yelled, rushing to where Shenandoah lay.

"Get some tea, fast," she ordered. Pouring oil out of the lamp into the palm of her hands, Miss Gibson rubbed it on Shenandoah's frail chest. She leaned over her. Then cupping her hands around Shenandoah's lips, she puffed air into her mouth.

"What are you doing, Miss Gibson?" I cried.

In between puffs she would rub Shenandoah's chest again. "I saw an old medicine woman. . . ." She puffed and puffed, then rubbed again, "I saw her save a baby whose heart had stopped by blowing air into her lungs."

When she stopped her rubbing motion to puff, Josh Paul was already there, puffing slowly into Shenandoah's mouth as he had seen Miss Gibson do. Miss Gibson kept rubbing her chest while Josh Paul blew air into her lungs.

Remembering the last words I had screamed at Shenandoah, I just sat there and cried. She was so good. She never complained. Never asked for anything. All she asked for was a Christmas tree. Mama promised next year we'd have more than a tumbleweed tree. She promised a real one, and Mama always kept her promises.

At Christmas, I could think of a million things I wanted. But now, all I wanted was to tell my sister I loved her.

Minutes ticked away like hours as Miss Gibson rubbed the oil on Shenandoah and Josh Paul puffed air into her face. Then, I saw a flutter in her eyes. They slowly opened, their pale blue blinking back at me. I wanted to blurt out how sorry I was for saying I hated her. I didn't.

"Don't you ever do that to us again!" I said.

"You looked like a goner to me!" Josh Paul swore. "It's a miracle, that's what it is." Tears stained his tan cheeks as his dark brown eyes seemed to pour love across Shenandoah's face. "I've never seen anything so amazing in my life."

"You're right, Josh Paul," Miss Gibson laughed as she tried to rub her own neck and shoulders, pulled tight and tense. "It's truly amazing."

Shenandoah spoke in a breathless whisper, "I could see you." Even though she was pale, her face glowed as she spoke. "I remember thinking how much y'all loved me to work so hard. I could hear you thinking, Shyanne."

"You always could," I answered.

"Never like this time. You were thinking of Christmas, next Christmas and how Mama promised us a real Christmas tree."

I choked back the emotion in my throat.

"I remember the one we had in Virginia," Shenandoah said. She could remember everything. Mama said Shenandoah's life was so fragile she had to enjoy each day as if it was a fine piece of chocolate to be savored slowly.

"A little fat tree with ribbons and lace and sweets tied to it." The look in her eyes spoke of long ago or maybe of what she saw in the future. Whichever, her thoughts weren't with us.

A tear lay on Josh Paul's cheek, but his smile reached from ear to ear. "We can just have Christmas right here, smack in the middle of February," he said in a burst of energy.

Miss Gibson dabbed at her eyes. "Certainly, we can!" she laughed.

"We can make a tree out of the benches." Josh Paul stood and started to pull them together, but Miss Gibson laid a hand on his arm.

"No, this has to be a real tree," she said.

"There's not a tree for twenty miles except ones someone planted." Josh Paul said thoughtfully.

"And the only one close is your tree you brought all the way from Tennessee." I looked at Miss Gibson, who was smiling. "Not your tree!" I whispered.

Miss Gibson motioned for us to be quiet, put on her coat and picked up an axe from the cupboard. Josh Paul grabbed his coat, too. Together, they opened the door. Clutching the rope they had tied to the shed, they struggled out into the storm.

Shenandoah slept. The storm howled outside the window.

After fifteen minutes, I got worried. People could freeze if they were out any longer. As I picked up a blanket to put over the coat I now wore constantly, I heard them coming back.

"This has got to be the coldest day in Texas," Josh Paul complained again.

"For once I agree with you, Josh Paul." Miss Gibson held her beautiful tree in her hands. Its trunk looked more like it had been chewed instead of chopped. There wasn't a trace of regret on her face. "Shiloh, you get the candle nubs we've been saving," Miss Gibson whispered as she opened boxes and drawers in her desk. "Josh Paul, get that last apple out and polish it."

"Those dried flowers on your desk would sure look pretty,"

he said cautiously.

"No!" I almost shouted. "Those are from your home place, Miss Gibson."

"This is my home now, Shiloh." She spoke as she handed Josh Paul the flowers and continued to fashion an angel out of the handkerchiefs she had stored in her desk. "We can't hold on to the past or cry over its sorrows. We have to make today count."

I glanced at Shenandoah and promised myself I'd apologize to her before I went to sleep.

As we lit the candles and placed the angel on top of the tree, we stepped back to view our handiwork. It was a beautiful tree.

"Shenandoah," I shook her gently. "It's Christmas." She woke. Her smile brightened the room.

"I know it's not December," she said as she looked around. "But I feel like it's Christmas." I helped her sit up so she could get a better view.

"It's beautiful," she whispered. The tree's image reflected in her eyes. "I am so lucky."

Miss Gibson reached for her dulcimer. She played "O Tannenbaum, O Tannenbaum," and Josh Paul and I sang.

After the singing, I gave Shenandoah some broth Miss Gibson had made out of beef jerky. Her strength spent, I gently laid her down. Quietly we watched the candles burn as low as possible without catching the tree on fire.

It was the best Christmas ever. I slipped under the cover next to Shenandoah. As I drifted off to sleep, I remembered it was February the eleventh, three days before Valentine's Day.

I woke up shivering in the early dawn. I thought I heard a sound. I lay listening, waiting. Then I realized, the lack of sound had awakened me.

The storm was over. With the calm came a cold that shook me to the bones. I snuggled under the blanket, pulling its tattered edge up over my nose.

The strange silence bothered me because it was more than the wind stilled. Shenandoah's raspy breathing didn't fill the room. I sat up and checked my sister's forehead for a fever, as Mama had taught me.

She was cold. She wasn't breathing. This time I knew there would be no miracle, and I hadn't told her I loved her.

Chapter Four

I felt alone. For the first time in my life I didn't feel bound by that cord of shared emotion, that feeling of being a twin.

I shook Miss Gibson and Josh Paul, but I didn't say anything. There wasn't anything I could say.

Miss Gibson woke with a start. She tried to rub on Shenandoah's chest but quickly gave up with a deep sigh. "She's gone."

All I could muster was a nod. The rest of the day I managed to respond to Miss Gibson's kindness with "No, thank you," and "Yes, ma'am, I'm fine." Josh Paul didn't speak, but he and Miss Gibson cried. I couldn't cry. Crying would have made me feel better, and I didn't deserve to feel better.

Hours later when Josh Paul tried to open the door it didn't budge. His brown eyes flashed a worried look at Miss Gibson. She went over to help force the door, but it held fast.

Josh Paul ran to the window. It was packed shut with solid ice and snow. He pried it open a few inches and stuck a fire poker into the ice, trying to break it away from the window. Then he sank onto the bench in despair. The poker only made a small tunnel through the snow. Unable to reach the cow chips for the fire, we broke up benches or anything else that would burn.

I tried not to think of Shenandoah's body wrapped and stored in the cloakroom, far from the heat of the fire. When Grandpa died, Grandma had dressed him in his best suit. The hand-carved wooden coffin was placed in the parlor. Friends and neighbors came to visit, bringing food by the wagon loads.

Everyone stood over Grandpa and said what a nice long life he had had.

Here, Shenandoah was separated from the warmth of home and family. And if we talked about her life, it would have to be about how short it had been. Slowly, Josh Paul began to talk about Shenandoah. He and Miss Gibson remembered her kindness and sweet ways. Not me. I didn't want to remember. To me, each memory was a knife that sliced away part of who I was, because part of me was Shenandoah.

On the fourteenth day of February, we sat around pretending not to be sad or hungry. Suddenly, we heard a scratching.

"Someone's digging," Miss Gibson said, lighting up with optimism.

I hoped it wasn't Mama. I couldn't face her with the fact I hadn't taken care of my sister.

"Miss Gibson?" Mr. Walsh's voice filtered through a yard of snow.

"Yes, we're here!" Miss Gibson yelled.

"We'll have you out in no time," he answered.

We carried Shenandoah's lifeless body, wrapped in Miss Gibson's favorite quilt, out into the light.

Miss Gibson answered Mr. Walsh and Mr. Younger as they whispered questions about Shenandoah. They took Shenandoah's body and placed her in the back of Mr. Younger's sleigh.

"I'm mighty sorry, Shyanne." Mr. Younger hugged me and then laid a rough work-worn hand on Josh Paul's shoulder, pulling him close. "Are you okay, son?" Josh Paul nodded.

Mr. Walsh took Miss Gibson's arm. "I'll take you to the boarding house, ma'am." Mr. Walsh moved the fur covers he had in his sleigh to the side and placed the mail bag over in the middle to make room for her.

Josh Paul, Miss Gibson and I looked at one another. We couldn't say good-bye like we usually did. We had shared laughter, hunger, fear and death. It hurt to leave each other.

Miss Gibson pulled us into her arms and said, "I couldn't have survived without you two. You were so strong."

"Thank you," I whispered, my eyes burning but dry. What I needed was to spill out my emotions in torrents of tears, but I couldn't give myself the pleasure. I didn't deserve tears. I deserved the pain in my chest, the constant hollow feeling of loss.

Mr. Younger, Josh Paul and I crowded into the front of the two-seater wagon. Long planks of lumber attached to the wheels turned the wagon into a sleigh. Feller resembled a strange animal from a foreign country. His hooves were wrapped in rabbit fur, a burlap sack covered his ears, and a saddle blanket warmed his back under his harness. Mr. Younger snapped the reins to encourage the horse to move faster.

"Lon Mulhall, who runs the weather station, says it got down to twenty-three degrees below zero the other night." Mr. Younger's words smoked into the frigid air.

Josh Paul's red head popped up from under the quilts. "That low? You don't say?" he said with a shiver. "It felt colder than I ever remembered."

"I think that's colder than any of us ever remembered." Mr. Younger spoke as he pulled his scarf over his mouth.

Sinking back into the furs, Josh Paul added, "Coldest day in Texas."

I silently agreed.

The wind hurt my lungs. The Texas sun that scorched the land in July and August was hard pressed to melt even one snowflake. Country that had become so familiar we could have felt our way across it on a moonless night now sloped at unusual angles. Dugouts were large frozen dunes topped with chimneys of smoke. Tracks trailed out from high windows and led to livestock or fuel.

"It's beautiful, isn't it?" Josh Paul glanced over the fields. His brown eyes appeared cinnamon in the glare of the sun.

"Shenandoah would have loved this," I said. "All the ugly stuff covered up."

"It must be a little like heaven." Josh Paul turned toward me, his face drawn so close by the blankets I could feel his breath, warm on my cheeks.

"I don't believe in heaven anymore," I said, keeping my eyes on the trail ahead.

"You don't believe in heaven?" he asked.

I hated to answer him. Josh Paul loved causes. He'd be after me like a hound dog after a rabbit from now on. "No!" The words became unripe grapes in my mouth and had to be spit out. "I don't believe in heaven, happy-ever-after, or hoping for things to turn out good."

"Shyanne, there has to be a heaven!" Josh Paul said with an aggravated look on his face. "People like Shenandoah are too much alive to disappear. She has to be someplace wonderful."

I bit on the side of my mouth and considered that thought. I knew my sister had to be someplace, someplace beautiful and sparkling like the snow-covered prairie before me. "Yeah, I guess you're right," I answered. "Shenandoah is in heaven." I could almost hear her laughing and singing. "But, I'll never hope for miracles or believe in that happy-ever-after malarkey again."

The runners of the homemade sleigh whispered as we swished across the miles home. Josh Paul turned around ten minutes later as if we had been talking only seconds before and added, "But, Shyanne, you have to have hope. After all, Shenandoah did come back to life once. That was a miracle."

"That was a fluke—a waste!" My voice shook with anger. "It's all for nothing—the tree, the second chance with Shenandoah—nothing, except to get our hopes up and dash them to the ground."

"Just because one time turns out unhappy, you can't stop hoping." Concern filled his eyes. "You never know when a miracle can happen."

"Believe me, Josh Paul, miracles don't happen." I turned my back. I wanted to shut out his voice and the thoughts, even the road before us that led home—home where Mama waited for Shenandoah.

"Then I guess we'll have to wait until another miracle comes along that'll make you believe," Josh Paul said, poking me as he spoke each word. I turned and glared at him.

"If we don't move again this year, I might believe in miracles. If Mama doesn't have another baby this year, it would sure enough be a miracle. That's happened four of the last five years." I sighed, "No, I don't believe in miracles."

We drove in silence the rest of the way to my house. It wasn't really a house like we had had in Arkansas. It was a half-dugout. Half buried in the ground to keep us warm in winter and cool in summer. Shenandoah had a way of describing it that brought a beautiful three-story mansion to mind.

We pulled up to a large hill of snow with a chimney puffing out black smoke. I wouldn't have recognized it if Mr. Younger hadn't stopped the wagon and pulled out his shovel to clear the snow from the door. The dugout faced south so it didn't take long.

Pa's voice cut through the silence. His ranting and raving embarrassed me more than I thought possible. Mr. Younger helped me down from the sleigh.

"Most fathers sound a lot like grizzly bears after being cooped up with a herd of kids for a week," he said. "I expect you'll want to talk to your folks alone."

I would have loved Josh Paul for his pa alone in hopes he'd grow up to be as good and kind.

"Don't want visitors." Papa's voice, heavy with what he called medicine, floated through the straw stuffed cracks of the walls. He stumbled to the door and peeped out. "I figured you two would come sashaying home after your ma's near killed herself doing your chores during the storm." Before Papa started drinking, he had been kind and hard working. However, that had been so long ago, I barely remembered.

Josh Paul and his father pretended not to hear Pa.

"We couldn't get home, Papa." I tried to explain.

"Where's the puny one?" he growled.

I tried to speak, but the words seemed to be barricaded behind an icy wall of emotions.

"Shenandoah got mighty sick, Mr. Jones." Josh Paul stepped up beside me and put his hand on my shoulder.

"I hope you didn't pile up a doctor bill. I can't afford doctors," Papa grumbled.

Mama pushed Papa away. She looked weary. Her blue eyes, so much like Shenandoah's, sparkled with happiness when she saw me. But the highlights quickly faded. She frantically searched for Shenandoah before her gaze finally stopped on the small bundle lying in the back of the sleigh.

I had never seen Mama cry. Today her hands trembled, and she swayed so I was afraid she would faint. One slender hand grasped the rough beams supporting the dugout porch, but she didn't cry.

"I'm sorry, Mama. I tried to help her. We all tried to help her. Miss Gibson saved her one time when she stopped breathing. It just wasn't enough." My voice sounded like someone else's. I didn't cry either. I couldn't.

Josh Paul reached out to steady Mama. She took a gulp of the frigid air and plowed through the snowdrift toward the sleigh. Her hand caressed the still bundle that held Shenandoah. Then, she tried to lift her. Quickly, Mr. Younger stepped up to help her.

Mr. Younger carefully carried Shenandoah into the house. Josh Paul helped Mama inside. Papa stood in the middle of the room, his eyelids heavy and his mouth open. The boys grabbed me in a hug that felt more like tug of war.

"You're home! You're home!" Augusta shouted.

"Hurray! Hurray!" Jackson chimed in.

"Hooway! Hooway!" Murfrees mimicked his brother and Russell added strange variations of welcome.

"Where's 'Doah?" Jackson suddenly stopped hugging me and looked past Mr. Younger and Josh Paul. "'Doah! I want 'Doah," he cried. Jackson always did want Shenandoah.

"Hush!" Mama warned. She pushed the dirty dishes off the table into the wooden washing tub. "You'll wake the baby."

Mr. Younger gently laid Shenandoah on the table.

"Thank you kindly for bringing my girls home, Mr. Younger." Mama's voice remained soft and low, but she stood tall and straight.

"You're welcome, ma'am. The ground's too frozen for a funeral, but Mrs. Younger will be happy to come over and prepare the body for burial," he offered as he stroked the quilt with a rough hand. "Can I do anything else?"

"No, I can manage. Thank her, though." Mama said, moving and talking as if she was baking a batch of corn pones. Her self-control amazed me.

"You'll want to prepare her now." Mr. Younger struggled to keep his emotions out of his words. "I'll make a box for her."

Mama nodded. She unwrapped the quilt from Shenandoah as if it were lace around fine crystal. "We'll get her looking her best and then place her body in the root cellar until the ground thaws."

I couldn't bring myself to think of Shenandoah down in that cold, dark root cellar.

Mr. Younger walked to the door. Josh Paul shyly patted my hand and turned to follow his pa. I wanted to say good-bye, but my mind, like my emotions, was as frozen as the Texas prairie. I heard the door click behind them.

Jackson put down the home-made toy he was taking apart and asked, "What's that, Mama?" He stretched to see what lay in the bundle.

"It's Shenandoah, honey," Mama whispered.

Murfrees pulled his thumb out of his mouth and asked, "When will her wake up?"

Mama filled the wash bowl with water. "She's not asleep. This is not the part of Shenandoah you loved. This is just her body that got all worn out and sick. The part of your sister that loved and laughed is in heaven."

"You mean, she won't live in her body here with us?" Augusta stopped arranging his collection of Indian arrowheads and got that thoughtful look on his face—the one that sparks his bright little mind into asking a thousand questions.

"No, Shenandoah has a new body, now." Mama's lip quivered, but she continued to work without a tear. "You remember the larva we found last spring?"

Jackson shook his head no.

"The worm you put in the box." Augusta was quick to explain. "We fed it dill weed."

The light of understanding sparked in Jackson's brown eyes. "He spinned a cocoon."

"The worm formed a chrysalis." Mama washed Shenandoah as though she were a china doll.

"I remember." Jackson made a butterfly motion with his hands. "The butterfly flew away!"

"I 'member too," Murfrees echoed.

"No, you don't!" Jackson argued. "You always have to say whatever I say."

I touched tow-headed Murfrees, enjoying the feel of his soft white hair and said, "Hush, you two."

"I don't want him saying what I say." Jackson pushed on Murfrees' shoulder.

"No fighting, boys." Mama's voice grew faint, lost in memories. "Shyanne, can you get your sister's Sunday dress?"

I rummaged in the chiffonnier, opening the drawers on one side and then the door on the other until I found the pink and gray dress. I listened to the rest of Mama's explanation as carefully as the boys.

"The larva is no longer a worm. It becomes a butterfly and leaves the empty chrysalis—cocoon. This isn't Shenandoah anymore." Mama said. "This is like a chrysalis and Shenandoah is like the butterfly. She has a new body and is flying all over heaven."

"Like in the song?" Augusta broke his thoughtful silence. "I'm gonna fly all over heaven," he sang.

Jackson joined in the gospel song in a loud voice. "Heaven, gonna fly all over God's heaven. . . ."

"Stop that singing!" Papa grumbled from his bed. Then turning to face the wall, he covered his head with a pillow and started to snore. I had never hated him as much as I did at the moment.

Jackson and Augusta stood on their knees on the only bench close to the table. After trying to make room beside them, Murfrees dragged a box up nearby. I stepped between the boys to prevent a fight. Mama gave me a smile.

She changed Shenandoah into her Sunday dress and brushed her hair. Mama's lips drew tight and her face paled when she tied a pink ribbon around Shenandoah's golden curls.

"Can I go to he'ben, too?" Murfrees asked.

Mama put her arm around him. "We'll all go, someday, but you still have butterflies to catch and cookies to eat."

"Cookies?" all three asked hopefully.

"Can we have cookies now?" Jackson asked.

"One for each hand." Mama smoothed their hair and wiped their noses, then handed them two cookies each.

Long after we said good night and the boys were asleep, I lay awake thinking about Shenandoah's body all bathed in candle light. I tried to imagine her new body. Mama's butterfly story may have helped the boys, but I felt like I was the empty shell of the cocoon.

A long time later, I heard Mama weeping softly.

Chapter Five

Mr. Younger returned early the next day with a box he had converted into a casket for Shenandoah. Mrs. Younger had lined it with a quilt made of dainty print scraps. When they placed Shenandoah's pale body into the box, my heart seemed to float in with her. And when Mr. Younger nailed the lid shut, muscles in my neck and back jerked with each blow of the hammer.

By nightfall the box was in the root cellar, and we had returned to the routine of life, almost as if Shenandoah never was. Yet the dugout seemed to ring with her soft laughter.

My brothers talked about her as if she would come in the door at any moment. Augusta was nervous and jumpy. His eyes wandered to the door of the root cellar and lingered there. It was his first experince with death, and I remembered that fear. When Grandpa died, I had been afraid to sleep. The place where his casket lay on Grandma's big oak table was clearly in my view, and I shook then the way Augusta was shaking now. Shenandoah had put her arms around me and told me stories of angels.

I sat down beside Augusta, but I felt awkward trying to put my arm around him. Shenandoah's arm had naturally curved around others. The best I could manage was to pat his knee. It seemed to calm him.

"You know Sister's dancing with the angels now," I stammered. Augusta nodded. His eyes were larger than usual, and I could see the Adam's apple in his thin neck move as he swallowed.

"But," he whispered, "I thought I saw her eyes move."

He waited for me to say something, but I didn't know exactly what to say. "Just before Mama wrapped her up and put her in that box," he muttered.

"No, she's dead," I said. "Mama would never put her in a casket if she wasn't sure." I brushed a lock of sun-streaked hair from his brown eyes. "She's dancing on clouds and chasing angels from star to star. Sometimes they let special people play with them."

"Sister was special," Augusta added.

"Yes," my voice caught. Behind the words, pent-up tears waited to spill out. "She was special."

🌹 🌹 🌹

"Shiloh Anne!" Papa's voice shook me awake the next morning. "That cow's got to be milked and fed, and you boys need to fetch more chips from the shed." Papa barked orders and then took another dose of his cough medicine. I knew it was homebrew. The brew was a problem, but when he ran out of it, he acted even meaner.

Augusta jumped and began to shake again.

As I bundled up in an extra layer of clothes and went out to milk old Sally, I thought about Papa. I wondered how he felt about Shenandoah. What made him so mean? Older than Mama, he had been a fine gentleman before his family lost their plantation in the War between the States.

Outside, sunlight kissed the great white ocean of snow that lay before me. Wave after wave of drifts winked back the sunlight. A small hole in the wall of snow was where our barn had been. I looked close and saw Sally's nose peeking through. Her warm breath made an opening in one of the many places the barn needed repair.

Inside, the barn was as warm as one of the igloos Miss Gibson said they have up north in Seward's Folly. I nudged Sally over and placed the stool at her flank. Taking off my gloves, I washed my hands in some snow. Then I rubbed them together to warm them before I touched Sally's teat. She still sidled away from me, but I spoke soothing words. I placed Sally's udder between my thumb and palm of both hands, squeezed and tugged downward.

The milk made a squirt-plink sound as it hit the bucket. I usually hated milking, but today Sally seemed to understand my mood. She swished her red spotted tail and blinked her big brown eyes in sympathy.

"Sally, I've made a mess of things for sure." I spoke softly as I milked. "You wouldn't believe the ugly words I said to Shenandoah."

Sally turned her head and looked at me.

"Maybe you would. I guess I've lambasted you a time or two."

Sally slowly chewed as I talked, then turned her head back to the hay trough.

"I hate myself, and I'm ashamed of Pa. We both deserve to lose Shenandoah, but not Mama or the boys." I cried gently into Sally's soft brown hide. She gave an understanding "moo." By the time I had finished milking, Sally and I both felt better. I threw hay into the corral for the rest of the herd and slowly walked inside.

🌹 🌹 🌹

Waiting for twenty inches of snow to thaw can be a long wait, especially when the temperature is lower than the backside of a prairie dog's tail. Supplies were short, but Papa wouldn't move until he ran out of "medicine."

It was an afternoon toward the end of February when Mama told me to go in to town with Papa and bring back some flour and salt. Even though Papa protested, I swung up on the back of his horse.

"Why does a grown man have to have a snip of a girl tagging along? I can pick up supplies and get home in half the time without her," he griped.

Ma winked at me and tucked a hankie in my pocket. In it would be the coins needed to buy supplies. I knew not to tell I had it. Mama guarded the small amount of cash she received from her mother. It wasn't enough to keep us from starving, but it helped.

"Shyanne," Mama said, "tell Mr. Walsh to plan Shenandoah's services for Sunday." Turning to Papa she warned, "You just see that you have this child home before dark, Henry Jones, or don't come back. I'll not bury two daughters!"

"Hold your tongue, woman!" Papa raised his hand then stopped. His red-rimmed eyes glared with rage. Slowly, he lowered his hand and cursed loudly. "A grown man! Females bossing me at every turn." He pulled his tattered gentleman's hat down over his eyes to block the sun reflecting off the snow. "This is still a man's world unless the war changed that, too." He kicked the side of his stallion, Rebel-Call, with the heel of his worn boots.

Rebel came with us from Georgia. Mama said he had been bred from a long line of prize horses that once belonged to the Joneses. My grandfather, Jacob Jones, made two fortunes, one in cotton on the plantation where Papa was born and the other by blockade running during the war with the North. President Abraham Lincoln had Union ships guard southern ports to prevent the South from selling crops. Then they couldn't afford an army. But the Confederacy outran the blockade, and men like my grandpa sold their crops at higher-than-ever prices. Both fortunes Grandpa made had been used to spoil his three children.

When I would get angry with Papa, Mama would remind me of how hard the war had been and how it had left Papa bitter on life. Before the war, he had been the son of a rich man. He saw his house burn, his land go for taxes, and his father kill himself. Rebel was all he had left. Papa often said, "With the defeat of the

36

South came bad luck." He blamed everything on the war. To hear him talk, a person would think the war was a thing of the present. But the South had been defeated over thirty years before, and Papa couldn't let it end. The war was still being fought, but it raged inside him.

The trip to town was fast paced. I clung to Papa's back, using his broad shoulders for a shield against the cold wind. Papa barely stopped to let me slide off Rebel's back at Bulews' store.

"Be here waiting for me." His voice was gruff.

"How long?" I called after him, but he rode off without an answer. I stood by a drift of snow in front of the store and watched him gallop away.

There were other stores in Tulia—General Mercantile and a new one owned by Mr. Cantrell, but Mama had always done business with Bulews'. They let us buy on credit when Grandma's money was late arriving.

I walked up the steps and slipped into the store. Its fire warmed my hands, while its spirit warmed my heart. Much of its warmth was from the kind heart of Maybell Bulew. Much of its clutter was due to Herschel Bulew.

"Shyanne Jones," Mrs. Bulew folded me in one of her bearhugs that left a body gasping for air but made you feel definitely welcomed. "We didn't know if you folks were well." She ran her hand over my bangs and tossed my pigtails back over my coat. "I'm sorry about your precious sister. How is your ma holding up?"

"You know Mama. She takes whatever with a smile and says, 'Thank you, Lord.'" My voice sounded skeptical.

"That ma of yours does have grit." Mrs. Bulew crushed me against her large frame again. Then she ambled back to her work, moving from shelf to shelf, spacing the merchandise out over the empty areas.

"From the looks of the store, the snow's slowed Josh Paul's uncle in making his freight runs," I said, hoping to change the subject. Mr. Bulew came down the stairs from the loft they called home.

"Almost everyone counts on those supplies from Clarendon," he said. "How are the Joneses?" He was as much a contrast with his wife as a sugar ant is to a honey bee. He worried and worked, getting nowhere, while Mrs. Bulew soared though the wildflowers life offered as if she had wings, instead of a body three times the size of her husband's. She fluttered from person to person, gathering and spreading sunshine.

"Half the county is sure to pull up stakes when the trail thaws." Mr. Bulew predicted his doom almost with delight.

"Herschel, today half the county's been in here buying everything we have in stock. Believe me, they're staying." Mrs. Bulew threw her hands up in the air. "Don't get yourself all worked up until the fat hits the fire."

"That's what worries me. Business is just too good to last," her husband grunted back.

I handed her the money tied up in the kerchief. "Mama wants flour and salt, please, ma'am."

"I'll have it ready in a wink." She sat the jars of canned goods down on the counter and wrapped up my order in a small package, securing it with string.

"I'm not in a hurry." I looked at the tall jar of licorice sticks beside the cash drawer. "Papa said I had to wait outside for him."

"Outside?" Mrs. Bulew placed her chubby hands on her rotund hips. "Lawdy, child, as cold as it is?"

"I'll be fine. I'm all bundled up," I explained.

"You just un-bundle and I'll watch for your pa," she ordered as she counted out my change and tied it back in the kerchief.

"No, ma'am, I better be outside waiting the minute he rides up. Besides, I have to speak to Mr. Walsh about the funeral."

Mr. Bulew sat by the fire waiting for his companions of doom to show up for their day of "predictions" and "I told you."

He looked at me and shook his head. "You'll die out there, and then your ma will have two frozen corpses and two graves to dig."

"Herschel!" Mrs. Bulew's voice rose in anger.

Her husband stood and shuffled over to get his pipe from the mantle. "I'm just stating the obvious."

"Well, don't," she said, placing her arm around me. "And don't you pay any attention to him, Shyanne." She gave me a squeeze. "When do you expect to have the funeral?"

"Mama says the ground will surely thaw enough by Sunday," I answered, wanting to change the subject.

"I expect she's right. Half the county will be there and of course the church choir will sing." Mrs. Bulew worked as she talked.

"Yeah, and they'll be feuding and fighting just like always," he interrupted. "The fence-makers and the fence-breakers, the big ranchers and the little ranchers, farmers and sheepmen."

For once he was probably right. Everything was at war with everything else on the prairie. The ranchers and squatters, like us, fighting over cheap government land. The jackrabbits battled the grasshoppers to see who could eat the garden first. The north wind battled the south wind, bringing hail and droughts to drive everything else away.

The brass bell above Bulew's door jangled. Priscilla Babcock and her little sister, Abigail, strutted in wearing new coats and scarves.

"We need two large screw-eyes, Mr. Bulew," Priscilla said.

"Is your pa building something today?" Mr. Bulew asked as he ambled over to his hardware supplies.

"Father ordered a sled for us from Chicago." Priscilla prissed over to the counter and plucked five sticks of licorice from the candy jar. We called her Prissy at school because she always bragged and acted as if she was better than everyone. Shenandoah had made excuses for her and said Prissy actually was afraid people didn't like her.

"That's pretty dumb," I laughed, "since there isn't a hill for forty miles."

"I know there's not a hill, silly." Prissy rolled her eyes and brushed me off. "Father's hooking the sled up to the horse and pulling us through the snow."

"What fun!" Mrs. Bulew said as she carefully wrote the purchase down in a big ledger.

I watched Prissy and Abigail rush out the door and wished I had a sled. I sighed. Even if I did have one, my papa wouldn't pull me around in the snow.

Mrs. Bulew picked the last few sticks of candy out of the jar. "This candy's getting old, don't you think, Herschel?" Wrapping them in brown paper, she handed them to me. "Here, Shyanne. You take these to your little brothers. There's six pieces. You better have one for yourself, so they won't fight."

I knew Mama wouldn't like my taking charity, but I did want a taste of the sweet black candy. "Thank you, ma'am."

Remembering Papa, I gathered my packages.

"Don't stay out there too long, young lady," Mrs. Bulew called as I closed the door and went down to Mr. Walsh's office. I gave him Mama's message, then waited by the hitching rail.

As soon as my eyes adjusted to the bright sun, I could see Prissy preparing for the sleigh ride. Mr. Babcock first pulled Abigail, then Prissy. As they circled the boarding house, Miss Gibson stepped out on the wide porch. Josh Paul was at her side. Prissy turned her head toward Josh Paul and fell off the sled, right at his feet.

"Careful, Priscilla," Miss Gibson said as she and Josh Paul helped Prissy to her feet.

"I can't imagine what threw me!" Prissy batted her eyes at Josh Paul. "I need someone to show me how to guide this sled," she said, smiling like a cougar in a hen house.

Mr. Babcock dismounted and ran to his daughter. "Are

you hurt, Sugarface?"

"I'm fine, Father." Prissy stood fluffing her red hair that stuck out from under her white fur hat. "However, I do need someone to teach me how to steer," the little liar purred.

"Your sister can help you, Sugarface," her father offered, but Prissy gave her father a mean look.

"Not Abigail, she'll kill us both." Then she turned back to Josh Paul, smiled and added, "I thought Josh Paul might ride with me." The little schemer looked down at the snow as if she hadn't planned it the minute she saw him.

I shrugged. Priscilla didn't know him like I did. He couldn't stand her, either, and he was too smart to fall for her flirty ways. Before I could finish my thought, Josh Paul got on the sled and wrapped his arms around the whiny, little flirt.

"That does it!" I mumbled as I turned back to Bulew's store. "Mrs. Bulew, I'm waiting for my papa down by the school," I shouted, then closed the door. I walked down Broadway not turning once to look at that traitor, Josh Paul. I could hear them laughing. Cutting across to the school, I thought I heard my name mentioned.

Dark shadows engulfed the school yard. I knew it was getting late, I missed my sister, and I was worried about Papa. He had had plenty of time to get his medicine from Old Man Tumphill. I tried to stay in the stream of sunlight for warmth, but it kept leaping farther and farther away. The sound of horse's hooves drew my attention to the other side of the school building.

"Shyanne Jones, what are you doing out here besides freezing that funny little nose?" Josh Paul slid off Feller and stood like he was king of the mountain, his hands on his hips.

"I'm minding my own business, thank you," I said as I walked toward the street. "I don't need help from Sugarface's boyfriend!"

"I'm not anybody's boyfriend anymore." He swallowed

the last word like it was a lump of coal. "I just wanted to ride that sled." He followed me as I paced along the road. "You should have stayed and taken a turn. It was fun."

"I wasn't invited. Besides, I wouldn't ride on her dumb old sled if it was the only one around."

"It is the only one around." He laughed at me. I ignored him. "What are you doing here?" he persisted.

"Waiting for Papa." I walked to the corner and looked both ways.

"Fine," Josh Paul marched up to the door and opened it. "Don't wait out here too long or that nose will fall off, especially the way you have it stuck up in the air." He walked in and slammed the door.

I heard him banging around in the schoolhouse. The banging was followed by a crash and a muffled curse word. I decided I better check on him before he tore the school apart. The room was tomb cold, the absence of desk and chairs a stark reminder of our ordeal just weeks before.

"I told Miss Gibson I'd clean up a little." Josh Paul had the ornaments off the tree, holding them gently in his hands. He placed them on the desk and quickly wiped at his nose.

"It was a beautiful Christmas tree," I said, touching the branches. The needles, dry and brittle, shattered in my hand.

"I better take it out before there are needles all over the building," Josh Paul said sadly as he maneuvered the tree outside.

"It's a shame it has to die. It was a beautiful tree," I said. "Beautiful things always die."

He set the tree down at the corner where he and Miss Gibson had cut it. "Things die, but life goes on. You should be grateful to still be alive after that storm, Shrimp. It's a miracle any of us survived."

"There you go with that miracle stuff again," I said, turning away in disgust.

He took me by the shoulders and turned me back around. "It was a miracle! Didn't you feel it?" His warm eyes bore a hole through me as he spoke. "Shenandoah had a few more minutes of happiness, and we had more time to let her know we cared about her."

Trying to forget the fact that I had let a second chance to tell my sister I loved her slip by, I stopped next to the little tree and turned my face away. I was angry with myself and that anger wouldn't go away. I let it spew out on Josh Paul. "Shenandoah is dead, just like this little tree and that's the way it'll always be. Nothing good will ever happen!"

"When will you get out of this ornery mood? It's hopeless thinking." He threw his arms up. "Hopeless thinking is a vicious circle. Every time you have those bad thoughts they are like arrows heading for a target."

"It sure beats being disappointed by that happy-ever-after stuff."

"What do I have to do to get you to stop looking for the bad?" He grabbed the tree and stabbed its gnawed trunk into the snow. "Do I have to make this tree come back to life to get you to appreciate the good things you've got?"

"Yep! Make that tree grow back." I glared at him. "I'd believe in your stupid miracles and happy-ever-after stuff then for sure." I walked out to the road mumbling, "That's just about the dumbest thing I've ever heard of, a cut tree growing back. Boys are so stupid!" I squinted in the late sun, searching for Papa.

Josh Paul stared at me. I didn't have to look. I could feel his eyes. A minute later, he walked over wearing a silly grin. "It's a deal."

"What's a deal?" I asked.

"The tree! It's going to grow back. You just have to believe." He jumped on Feller's back as I squinted up at him.

"I believe you're going mad!" I said. "Mad as Old Man

43

Bailford's dog." I watched for foaming at Josh Paul's mouth.

"You better come on with me, Shrimp. Your pa's not coming tonight." He stuck his hand out to help me up.

I tucked my head, wanting to argue. "Well, maybe if I stand here on this schoolyard and say, 'I believe my papa will come. I believe my papa will come,' he'll be here in a miracle-moment." I snorted a laugh. It was getting late, and ample time had passed for Papa to get his bottle and be well on his way to drunk. Josh Paul and I both knew Papa wasn't coming.

A muscle flexed in Josh Paul's jaw. I had won the argument. I grabbed Josh Paul's hand and pulled myself up on Feller. Huddling behind Josh Paul, I tried not to worry about Papa. He wouldn't be home until tomorrow, and he'd be meaner than a badger tied to a rattlesnake's tail.

Chapter Six

I was wrong. Papa didn't come home the next day, or the next. He didn't even come for Shenandoah's funeral. The morning of the funeral, we heard he had headed toward Fort Worth. Mama made more excuses for him, talking about the war and hardships. I was supposed to understand, but I didn't.

She wanted the funeral to be a happy one. She asked the preacher to talk about the beauty of heaven and how Shenandoah was running through fields of wildflowers, hand and hand with Jesus. When Mama talked about it, I could see heaven clearly.

The church was overflowing with mourners because the Bookout baby had also died during the storm too. Methodist, Baptist and Presbyterian all sharing the same building, packed in close with the men standing. This week it was the Methodist preacher, B. J. Jackson, who read the scripture.

"And I saw a new heaven and a new earth: for the first heaven and the first earth were passed away; and there was no more sea . . . ."

Jackson, Augusta and Murfrees wiggled in the space between Mama and me. Shawnee sat on Mama's lap and Russell on mine. I tried to listen as the preacher read the Bible's description of heaven.

"God himself shall be with them, and be their God. And God shall wipe away all tears from their eyes; and there shall be no more death. . . ." Reverend Jackson held his Bible high as he read.

I wanted to believe in a new earth without death, without

crying, an earth where papas didn't get drunk or hit people.

"Having the glory of God," the preacher continued, describing heaven, ". . . like unto a stone most precious, even like a jasper stone, clear as crystal; And had a wall great and high, and had twelve gates, and at the gates twelve angels . . . ."

I could see Shenandoah sitting on the gates with the angels, walking down the streets of gold, and just as quickly as I saw her, I knew I wasn't good enough for heaven.

"And there shall in no wise enter into it any thing that defileth, neither whatsoever worketh abomination, or maketh a lie: but they which are written in the Lamb's book of life."

The preacher's words were surely the answer. Telling your sister you hated her had to be an abomination, and I knew it was a falsehood. The gates of gold seemed locked up tight, and I was on the other side.

Reading from the gospel of St. John, the preacher's voice softened. "For God so loved the world, that he gave his only begotten Son, that whosoever believeth in him should not perish, but have everlasting life." He closed his bible. "Friends, this precious baby and this beautiful young girl are in the arms of God. This is our hope, that we can all share."

By the last prayer I just wanted to leave the church and go home. Instead, people got in their wagons to ride to the cemetery.

We rode by the courthouse in a line of wagons. A few salesmen at the hotel turned and took off their hats. You could hear their whispering of concern, the shake of their heads. I didn't want their pity. They didn't know Shenandoah. They didn't have the right to see our pain. I raised my chin higher and sat straighter.

Stark and barren, the cemetery stood off by itself. Yellow-brown blades of prairie grass blew in the brisk breeze, scraping against patches of snow. Mud and slush mixed to produce a drab-gray effect, coloring the cemetery dreary. Only the sun, warm on my face, spoke of life. I hugged Murfrees closer and closed my

46

eyes. If I tried I could pretend we were on a picnic, and Shenandoah was at my side.

Murfrees' wiggle brought me back to reality.

"You sleeping?" he asked.

"No," I answered, "just remembering." The sun was so bright I kept my eyes lowered. I kissed Murfrees' soft head and tried not to worry about the future. Papa had left before, but he had never stayed away this long.

Bill Atkins and four other men had come to the cemetery early and dug two graves—Shenandoah's and the Bookout baby's. The men were finishing the smaller grave when we arrived.

Mr. Atkins was a mighty nice fellow. He could tell stories of guarding Geronimo at Fort Sill. He had even made friends with Quanah Parker. A couple of years earlier, Mr. Atkins built fences around his land. Ben Rush, his neighbor, couldn't get to the cemetery or the courthouse. A feud had erupted between the two men, and they hadn't spoken since that time.

Here in the cemetery the two dug graves side by side. They were so covered in mud, it was hard to recognize them. Mr. Rush pitched his shovel up and tried to climb out of the hole, but the muddy area around the surface gave way, and he slid back down.

"Give me a hand," he called.

Mr. Atkins bent down and offered his hand. Mr. Rush took it and then looked up. They seemed to freeze in position, silently deciding whether to give or receive help.

Then Mr. Atkins tightened his grip, and Mr. Rush pulled up.

"Thanks, Bill," Ben Rush said giving Mr. Atkins' hand a firm shake.

I guessed fences seemed smaller when surrounded by death.

After prayers and a hymn, the men lowered Shenandoah's casket into the ground. Each person shoveled a small amount of the muddy earth in on top. It was good to think of Mama's butterfly story, to know Shenandoah wasn't in the cold ground but in heaven.

I looked up at the billowing white clouds above me. Maybe heaven was a gift. The funeral seemed soothing to Mama, but not to me. I felt worse.

* * *

A week rolled past with nothing but work and more work, as we cleaned up from the storm. Josh Paul stopped on his way to help rebuild the desk and boards we had burned at the school-house. Sometimes he'd bring us a pie or a stew from his mother. Mama and I planted Irish potatoes in the garden and black-eyed peas in shallow boxes in the barn. Then school started back up again.

I didn't think I would go since Mama needed my help, but she was up at dawn, packing my lunch.

"Education is your future, Shyanne," Mama said. "It's like a herd of cattle. You have to keep it growing, or you'll have nothing."

I could tell Mama was worrying about food. If we started killing our cattle we'd never be able to increase our herd. But Mama and I couldn't hunt. Papa had always done that.

She brushed her hair away from her forehead with the back of her hand and continued making biscuits for the boys' breakfast. "A herd won't do any good if we starve. Your Papa was going to buy some hogs and build me a smokehouse this spring." She paused, then sighed. "I'll ask Mr. Young to help me slaughter one of the heifers. We'll smoke and dry some of it into jerky. It'll last a spell." For all of her talk about faith without seeing and hoping for the best, Mama faced the truth when it was staring her in the face.

The truth was Papa wasn't coming home, and I didn't miss him as much as I should have. He had really left us a long time ago. But Mama remembered a man I didn't know.

She was an amazing woman. She had lost her husband and her daughter at the same time and still she found a smile for me and my brothers.

"Go learn as much as you can." She sent me out the door with a gentle shove.

The trail ahead looked lonely. I hugged my coat and tucked my head into the wind. A few minutes later, Josh Paul rode up behind me.

"Why didn't you wait for me at the rock, Shrimp?" He reached down to give me a hand up.

"I didn't know you wanted me to wait." I put my foot in the stirrup and pulled up on Feller.

"Well, now you know. A little shrimp like you shouldn't walk on the trail by herself," he ordered.

I grabbed hold of his coat and we rode in silence.

"Look! An eagle!" Josh Paul pointed to the sky where an eagle soared. Indians say that an eagle brings good fortune. "Maybe we can make a wish and it will come true." He closed his eyes. "I wish I could become a rich man!"

I wanted to make a wish. I wanted Josh Paul to think of me as his age instead of a little kid. I wanted him to let me be his equal. Mostly, I wanted him to stop calling me Shrimp. Yes, I wanted to a make a wish, but I didn't believe in wishing.

🌹 🌹 🌹

At school Shenandoah's empty seat haunted me all morning. Right before lunch, Miss Gibson moved us to different places in the room. She put me at the back, between Josh Paul and Prissy's best friend, Adele Johnson. Prissy was furious.

"I can't see this close," Prissy whined from the front row.

"Haven't you been sitting at the front all year?" Miss Gibson asked.

"Yes, ma'am, but my mother's been wanting to speak to you about that."

"Good! I'll go with you after school." Miss Gibson turned toward the board. "Perhaps you need eyeglasses."

Everyone snickered. Priscilla glared at me as Miss Gibson began the lesson.

"How much is nine times five?"

"Forty-five." The answer popped out of my mouth before I knew it was in my head. The entire class stared. Suddenly, I felt more weird than I did as dumb ole Shyanne.

"Shiloh, that's excellent. The nines are the hardest to multiply." Miss Gibson turned the class's attention away from me by declaring an extra five minutes for lunch.

"Smartypants," Prissy hissed as she brushed passed me and rushed to walk out the door with Josh Paul.

Tom Spencer ran by me, scattering my lunch and books. "You must be turning into a bookworm," he said.

"You sure look like one," Abigail chimed in.

Miss Gibson came over and sat on the bench next to me, and Tom and Abagail rushed on out. "Does that bother you, Shiloh?"

"Naw," I said, picking up my lunch, "Tom Spencer is a clod. He don't bother me."

"Doesn't." Miss Gibson corrected. "I'm proud of you for using your bright mind." She picked up my slate and handed it back to me. "Sometimes though, when a person we love dies, we think we have to live for them. So we start trying to act like that person, do as they did, be that person." She stood and walked to the chalk board, writing our spelling words as she talked.

"Shenandoah was a great person to pattern your life after, but you are a unique and wonderful person, too. No matter how excited I am that you have a new thirst for learning, I wouldn't want you to stop being you."

"I think being anything but me would be a big improvement," I said, staring at my reflection in my lunch bucket.

"You're a vivacious and delightful young woman. I wouldn't

want you to be any different!" Miss Gibson quickly added. "Other than make better on your grades."

"I'm the one that should have died." I spoke without any of the emotion I felt.

Miss Gibson left her work and came to me. "No, you shouldn't have, honey." Putting her arm around me, she continued, "I understand you feel this way, but the world needs you."

"You don't know me, Miss Gibson! You just don't know how awful I really am." I picked up my lunch and ran out.

Since the funeral, I had been doing all kinds of strange things, like listening, doing chores without complaining and singing the boys to sleep. I figured the more I did, the less I'd think about how I had hurt my sister.

Sitting behind the fuel house on a pile of cedar posts, I spread my lunch and just stared at it. I hated to eat alone. At least I was away from Prissy and Adele. A gust of wind blew my hair into my eyes. March wind had a lot in common with Prissy and Adele. The wind would stir up dirt anywhere, just like Prissy and Adele. But they were also the only two girls my age. Shenandoah would say that Prissy and Adele didn't want to be mean.

"Shrimp, what are you doing out here by yourself?" Josh Paul jumped up on the woodpile beside me.

"Eating," I answered sharply. "What do you think I'm doing?"

"And you're leaving me to hear Tom's rabid dog story all by myself." Josh Paul made his voice sound slow and outrageous like Tom's, then he changed his voice to sound shrill and whiny like Priscilla's. "And Prissy has a new dress that has to be the most expensive dress ever."

I laughed.

"Or have I gotten it mixed up?" Josh Paul clowned on. "Maybe it was Prissy's dress that was rabid and Tom's dog that was expensive."

I noticed Prissy strutting toward us and whispered,

"Speak of the devil."

"Josh Paul," Prissy called as she passed the corner of the shed. "Why did you leave? I was about to let you ask me to the April Fool's Day social at church."

"Funny you should mention that. I was just asking Shyanne to go with me and my folks," he answered.

Open-mouthed, Prissy stared at me. "Well, I never!" She stuck her nose in the air as she walked off.

Josh Paul and I pushed our noses up with our thumbs and mimicked, "Well, I never."

After we stopped laughing, I took a bite of my sandwich while Josh Paul talked.

"Have you heard from your pa?"

"Nope." I swallowed the dry biscuit.

"What's your mama gonna do?" He took out his knife and whittled on one of the logs.

"Just what she always does." Suddenly, I lost my appetite and threw my lunch back into the syrup can. I was humiliated. I didn't want to tell anyone the news, even Josh Paul. Facts were facts. Sunday everyone in church would know and by Monday the entire county would be shaking their heads and clicking their tongues.

"What does she always do?" Josh Paul asked again.

"She's going to have another baby!" I spit it out between clenched teeth.

"That's great!" He grinned, while I felt anger rise up in my throat.

"Great? Just how do you figure that, minnow brain? We don't have any money or food, and I'm the only one big enough to help."

"I mean, it's great the way you have so many brothers. I wish I had some." He tried to console me. "There will be food. There's the cattle, and the church will help."

"The Joneses don't take charity." I heard Papa's words

come out of my mouth as I jumped off the woodpile and walked over to the side of the school. I didn't like sounding like Papa, but I didn't want any charity either.

Josh Paul caught up with me. "I'm sorry," he apologized. I just meant your problems will work out."

"Is this another one of your hope-for-a-miracle speeches?" I kicked the dead tree he promised would grow back. "We'll have to move back to Grandma's and I'll have to be 'Grammy's sweet little lady' and learn how to serve tea, or we'll starve. It's that simple."

"Something will come up," Josh Paul said with a frown. Then he bent down and pushed the dirt back close to the tree trunk. "This tree is getting greener everyday," he said.

I started to laugh, then I glanced down. The tips of each branch were bright green. "That looks like paint to me." I said inspecting it closely. "What fool would paint a dead tree?" I asked without thinking.

"Paint? Can't you tell that's new growth?" he argued.

"Oh, brother!" I sighed. To add to all my troubles, my best friend had gone slapdab crazy.

After school, as we rode home, I realized painting that tree and pretending a miracle was Josh Paul's way of trying to cheer me. I felt that queasy feeling I had in February and smiled.

When I slid off Feller in front of my house, Josh Paul said, "See you Sunday."

I didn't want to see anyone on Sunday. The garden couldn't be planted for several more weeks. Even then, it could be killed by a late frost, hail, or eaten by rabbits. Our cellar shelves were bare. Sunday, Mama would stand up at church and praise God for His blessing, then ask for help and prayer. She had a lot of pride, but she wouldn't let her babies go hungry any more than she would let one of her neighbors go without. I would starve before I'd ask someone like Priscilla Babcock for a crumb.

The wind blew me the rest of the way home just about as

fast as I could have ridden. When I got within shouting distance of the dugout, Augusta and Jackson burst out the door, laughing and shouting, and jumped on my back, nearly pulling me down on top of them.

Inside the dugout, the smell of meat roasting over a mesquite fire coaxed me into a mouth-watering drool. Russell and Murfrees sat big-eyed, watching the roast turn brown. Their little tongues licked their sweet baby lips. I knew, right then, I'd beg or do anything else to keep them from hunger.

When Mama came in from the barn, I asked cautiously, "Did Mr. Younger kill a heifer, or did Papa come home?"

"No, he'll come home when he's ready," she answered, turning the meat.

Trying to hush the growling of my stomach, I asked, "Which heifer did you kill?"

"Mr. Conner sent this roast over from Tule Ranch. He said a steer got caught in a fence and had to be slaughtered. I knew it was just kindness, but I took it anyway. It's harder to take charity than to give it."

Mama looked better than she had in months. With her soft blond hair pulled back and tied at the nape of her neck, her blue eyes looked larger than usual. A touch of pink bloomed on her cheeks. She looked happy. All of us were happier without Papa, yet sad, the kind of sad you can't talk about without crying. Mama stopped fixing the cornbread and glanced at me. "I have a plan for some money," she said. "Do you mind missing school on Monday?"

Missing school one day wasn't my fear. I was afraid I'd have to quit completely and get a job or stay home with the boys. I guessed that's what she had in mind. She'd get a job and I'd stay home.

"On Monday," Mama continued, "I'll catch a ride into town with the mailman. By Monday night you can stop chewing on your fingernails, because there will be an answer to our problems."

"A miracle?" I grumbled.

"No. Not a miracle, a promise." She handed me the plates for the table and held on to them so I'd have to listen. "Why worry about what we are going to eat or wear? 'Look at the birds in the air; they neither sow nor reap and yet your heavenly Father feeds them.'" Mama often slipped Scripture into the conversation before we kids could stop listening. "'Consider the lilies of the field and see how they grow; they neither toil nor spin . . . . Will He not much more surely clothe you?'"

Mama took an iron skillet, put meat drippings in it, sprinkled flour and a dab of salt, then splashed in milk. Gravy, golden brown and bubbling, was ready in minutes.

"Shyanne, say the prayer," Mama asked.

"No," I answered, without any excuse. She didn't look at me as she set the gravy and meat on the table. I finished putting the forks and spoons beside the plates and quickly joined the boys.

"Murfrees, you offer thanks," Mama said, her disappointment reflected in her weary expression. Murfrees and the others quickly folded their hands and bowed their heads. I didn't do either.

"Thank you for sun and wain. Thank you, God, for eberything." He rushed to finish his prayer with a loud, "Mmmm, now!" instead of the "amen" he had been taught. His gray eyes met Mama's stern look, and he quickly tucked his head. "Amen," he whispered.

Mama's laughter broke the silence. "I suppose 'mmmm now' is an acceptable way to end a blessing."

Russell echoed, "mmmm," and we all laughed.

That laughter and roast would have to last us another week. Mama was sick Sunday morning, and a late cold spell kept us from walking to church. Monday, I stayed home as Mama had asked. She woke me around five. While we sipped coffee and nibbled on our pan toast, she told me, "I'll be in town by eight o'clock. I'll send a telegraph and while I wait for the reply, I'll attend the cattleman's association meeting."

"I didn't know women could go to the cattleman's association," I said holding my coffee cup like Mama held hers. Mine was filled mostly with milk.

"Lady ranchers do." Mama stood, washed her cup and folded her napkin. "I'll be home in time to fix supper." She was dressed in her best dress and only shoes. Both were patched—very carefully—but they were still patched. Someday, I promised myself, I'll make lots of money singing on one of those fancy riverboats and then I'll buy Mama new boots and twenty dresses.

"I'll have supper ready," I said.

"No, you'll have your hands full just looking after the boys." She laid her napkin on the cupboard. "Don't try to do anything else," she warned.

"We'll be fine, Mama," I assured her.

"I should have a hat." She looked in the mirror of the chiffonnier, stretching to see more of her dress. "A bonnet is the only hat I have, and that would never do for such an important job."

"What kind of job, Mama?" I asked, listing mentally all the jobs I could think of in the county. There were maids or cooks at the White Hotel, a clerk at one of the stores, but I couldn't think of much more.

"You just wait until I find out, worry-wart," she answered with a smile and then she walked out the door.

The memory of that smile spurred me on. It was one of those smiles that says, "I'm proud of you. You're growing up and I trust you." I piled my hair on top of my head like Mama sometimes did and surveyed my handiwork in the mirror. The mirror was supposed to reflect a beautiful lady. Instead a newly-hatched chicken with a patch of pin feathers on top peered at me. I jerked the pins out of my hair. "I'll never be pretty enough to be a singer on a riverboat." As I set the frying pan on the rack above the fire,

I tried to think of other ways to make money.

I mixed up a bowl of johnnycake batter, determined to make Mama proud of me. I had planned five projects to fill my day before the boys woke up with the rooster's crow. I began by dripping the johnnycake batter into the skillet in funny shapes.

"What's that?" Jackson asked as he scuttled down from the loft and looked into the skillet.

"It's a rabbit," I explained, bursting with pride at my delicious piece of art. "No plain old circle johnnycakes today, because I'm the mama."

Murfrees tiptoed out of his bed near the corner of the room. He had discovered his toes just after Thanksgiving time and tiptoed everywhere. "I want a wabbit," he said.

Russell toddled close behind, dragging his ragged blanket, the corner clutched tightly in his chubby little fist. His middle two fingers stayed firmly in his mouth. I took them out, but he put the left-hand fingers in their place. I decided anyone as quiet and good natured as Russell deserved to do anything he wanted. I placed the first johnnycake before him and made another for Murfrees.

"Mama makes plain round johnnycakes," Jackson said in a critical voice.

"I know, but today is your lucky day. I'm cooking."

A sleepy Augusta backed down the ladder from the loft as I began my next creation. "How about a bear?" I asked Jackson. He glared back at me through big brown eyes.

"I like round johnnycakes," he persisted.

Augusta rubbed his eyes and peered into the pan. "I want a snake."

"Snakes are too easy. How about a bear? Two big circles and small ones for legs, ears, and nose," I said as I poured in the batter. It didn't turn out exactly as I planned, and Jackson refused the plate with the peculiar looking johnnycake.

"I like Mama's johnnycakes." he said.

"Augusta, would you like a scary bear?" I used an excited voice to try to interest him in my johnnycake bear.

"Sure!" He took the plate with delight.

"I like plain round ones." Jackson tormented me.

"Well, I'll just fix myself a bull," I said temptingly. A big lump and a small one sizzled in the pan. I added horns and a tail, but as the batter spread, it took on the shape of an Indian, then oozed into a haystack-looking blob. Jackson rolled his eyes and placed his hands on his hips.

"That's no bull," he said.

"Don't complain," I warned as I flipped the cake over.

Jackson sat down in disgust. "Mama makes nice, round, johnnycakes."

I sighed, giving up on Jackson's spirit of adventure. "This nice, unusual, bull shaped cake is just right for a grown up." I used my most mature voice as I set the plate at my place. As I poured a round johnnycake into the pan, the baby's cry interrupted me. I quickly picked him up and cooed, "Good morning, Shawnee." His cry was a signal for a dirty diaper and if I didn't change it right away, he'd get diaper rash and cry for a week. Just then, Augusta yelled for me.

"Just a minute," I said, cleaning Shawnee's stinky bottom. His strong legs kicked and squirmed. He would be walking circles around Russell by summer. "You could have at least waited until after breakfast to do this," I teased my baby brother.

From the fireplace, Jackson made a casual announcement, "It's smoking."

Quickly slipping Shawnee down on a quilt, I raced to rescue my johnnycake.

"It's black," Jackson said through clenched teeth.

"No. It's just nice and brown," I explained.

"I don't like brown ones," Jackson sulked.

"More!" Murfrees cried.

"Actually, it's chocolate." I said. "A chocolate johnnycake."

"I don't like chocolate johnnycakes," Jackson cried.

"More, more, more! More!" Murfrees repeated. I set the burned johnnycake and the bull-Indian-haystack one down before Jackson.

"Take your choice or starve," I dared him.

He turned from the table in a pout.

A crash drew my attention from Jackson. Shawnee stood with a firm grasp on the cup towel that had been under the batter bowl. The mixing bowl was upside down on his head, batter dripping down his cheeks and onto his chubby little legs. He lost his balance and sat down on the floor with a scream.

"Oh, cow manure!" I scooped up the bowl in one hand and Shawnee in the other. His brothers joined in his scream of protest. "I'm going to tan your backsides if you don't hush," I yelled. "Augusta, you and Jackson get some water."

"Mama says it's too cold outside for us," Jackson answered.

"There's still big mounds of snow everywhere," Augusta chimed in. I put the bowl in the wash tub and Shawnee back on the quilt.

"Honestly, Augusta, a few patches of snow in the shadow of the barn." I picked up a damp cup towel and snapped it at their little bottoms. "Now you two do as I say!" Their eyes doubled in size and their feet danced to avoid the sting of my pop. They went, quickly. A wave of guilt washed over me as I cleaned up the mess and fed the baby. Mama wouldn't have lost her temper over something so unimportant. I vowed to spend the rest of the day being patient and kind.

Chapter Seven

Murder was more on my mind as I surveyed the mess around me. The older boys arrived with water, and I washed the dishes and rinsed off Shawnee. Then I filled the tub again, putting the diapers in to soak. Mama always scrubbed clothes, but it was my opinion if you just left them to soak, they'd clean by themselves.

Shawnee's eyelids grew heavy, and he tugged at the corner of his eyes. That meant it was already the middle of the morning. Shawnee was the best clock around and he didn't even tick. Russell tugged at my faded skirt, his big, dark eyes telling me lunchtime wasn't far away. I needed to get out of the house for a while, and the livestock needed tending. Not milked, Sally would be miserable by this time.

Then I had a stroke of genius. "A picnic. Let's have a picnic, boys."

Augusta and Murfrees were quick to agree, but not Jackson.

"It's too cold," he protested.

"Too cold," Murfrees echoed.

"I have to milk the cow," I told them, "and you all are going with me. Jackson, you and Augusta need to gather the eggs."

"Why do we have to do your work?" Jackson questioned my authority.

"Because I can't do everything." I shoved him toward his coat and hat, then packed a few slices of roast, bread and butter into a basket.

I wrapped the three little ones up and tied Shawnee to my

back, papoose-style. He had become much too quick to trust down on the ground. "You weigh a ton!" I told him as I shifted his weight to pick up the milk bucket and picnic basket. "Jackson, don't forget the egg basket."

Shawnee had to be corralled, so while the boys cleaned the stall, I put in fresh hay, then plopped Shawnee and Russell down on a horse blanket and shut the gate. Murfrees chased the chickens, while Augusta and Jackson gathered the eggs, resentment in every move. Before I sat down on the three-legged stool, I rubbed one of Sally's red and white ears. I placed the bucket between my knees.

The milk hit the bucket in the rhythm of a fast song. Some days I milked and sang slowly to avoid my schoolwork, but today I felt like a fast tune.

"Plant a watermelon vine up on my grave so the juice can . . ." I curled my tongue up against the roof of my mouth and inhaled. (Slurp! Slurp!) ". . . slip through."

Too soon, Jackson, Augusta and Murfrees interrupted my concert with fussing. "That's my egg," Jackson yelled.

"My egg!" Murfrees repeated.

"You have two already," Augusta complained. "I only have one."

Scuffling sounds came from the egg loft. "Well, I found it!" Jackson demanded.

"You two stop fighting, and I'll sing "Playmate." You like that song." I continued singing.

Hey, hey, hey, playmate,
Come out and play with me,
And bring your dollies three.
Climb up my apple tree,
Holler down my rain barrel,
Slide down my cellar door,
And we'll be jolly friends forevermore.

Hey, hey, hey, playmate,
I can't come out and play,
My dolly has the flu,
Boo, hoo, hoo, hoo, hoo, hoo.
Can't holler down your rain barrel,
Can't slide down your cellar door,
But we'll be jolly friends forevermore.

"Ow!" Augusta wailed. "Sister, help."

Augusta and Jackson landed in a heap at the bottom of the three steps that led to the hen roost. I set down my bucket and grabbed Murfrees off the top step. After I plopped him down in the corner, I grabbed Jackson's collar in one hand and Augusta's in the other to separate the two. Eggs were splattered all over both of them.

"Now, you've ruined the cake I was going to make," I scolded. "No eggs, no cake!" Just as I whacked them on their backsides, the baby cried. That spooked Sally, causing her to kick the milk bucket. I grabbed for it to save the milk from spilling, tripped on a hoe, and went sailing through the air. When I sat up I felt something warm and moist beneath my hand.

"Oh, cow manure!" I screamed. The boys ran, laughing.

Wiping as much of the nasty stuff off my hand as I could, I chased them to the house. As I hit the latch I heard the safety bar fall into place on the other side. The little devils had locked me out! Shouts of victory erupted from inside.

"Too bad you three won't get any lunch," I said. My rage took me quickly to get water from the trough to wash my hands.

In clear view of the window where the boys could see, the babies and I enjoyed lunch in the sunshine. I expected Augusta to open the door at any time. Instead, the shutters slammed shut.

After lunch, I beat on the door. They could tell I meant business when I used their second names.

"Augusta Lee, open this door!" I waited. "Jackson

Stonewall," I hissed. "You better open this door or you won't be able to sit on your sitter for a week!" I threatened.

When I got no response, I tried bribing Murfrees. "Murfrees, honey, do you want to go look for berries?" I coaxed through the door, knowing there wouldn't be any berries this side of the Rio Grande until late summer. "How about a handful of choke-berries to eat?"

Still no answer. I walked back to the babies, feeling as tired as they looked. "Let's go, babies," I yelled. "We'll eat all the berries."

I walked down the path leading to the creek, toting a baby on each hip. As soon as I was behind the barn, I sneaked in and put Russell and Shawnee back in their pen. We waited long past an hour before Murfrees' little tow-head poked out the door. He tip-toed to the path, trying to see where I might be. I seized the moment and ran for the door. The two older boys were sound asleep with their arms wrapped around each other in buddy fashion.

I wanted to strangle them, especially when I saw the lit-tle bit of left over roast, mangled beyond repair. But the quiet was too precious, so I got the babies and Murfrees and tucked them all in for a nap.

The room was a mess. I sank down on the rocker in despair. Moments later, I was fast asleep.

When I woke up, the sun behind the barn cast long rib-bons of dark shadows on the ground. Augusta and Jackson sat on the floor playing with the baby, behaving as sweet as angels attending baby Jesus. Sounds of a rider coming up the trail delayed my stern lecture. Josh Paul appeared at the door, carry-ing a pot of his Mama's stew.

"Hey, Shrimp. How ya' doing?" He looked more grown up than usual in a new shirt that matched his eyes. "Mama thought you might need this. She saw your ma at the cattleman's association. Your ma said she'd be later than she thought. You're not to worry and be sure to lock the door."

"How sweet of your ma." Self-conscious over what looked the biggest mess, the house or me, I raked my fingers through my hair and shoved the dirty dishes into the washing pan. Then I took the pot from him.

"Can you stay and eat it with us?" My voice surprised me—it sounded syrupy sweet, like Priscilla's. But Josh Paul came in and hung his hat like he didn't mind.

"Thanks, Shyanne. I sort of missed that funny little nose of yours at school today," he said timidly.

All during supper the boys were captivated by Josh Paul, and didn't cause one fuss. I knew it had to be a first for them not to fight or spill something. After Josh Paul helped me bathe all five of them and put them to bed, we each collapsed in front of the fire.

"Maybe it's best that I'm an only child," Josh Paul said.

As I looked into the fire I thought of how it would be if I was grown and Josh Paul was my husband. Dreamily I imagined him coming in the door, me stirring a pot over the fire and rocking a cradle with my foot.

The day flashed through my mind and I quickly decided I wasn't ready to be a wife and mother. "You should have been here this morning," I sighed as we watched the fire lick red and yellow tongues toward the blackened stones. "You'd never want children at all."

"Someday, I'll have a house in New York City, maybe become an actor," Josh Paul dreamed.

"And wear silk shirts?" I teased, knowing full well that he hated dandies that wore silk shirts.

He curled his lip and shook his head as if he was erasing the image of himself as an actor. "Maybe I'll join a wild west show. P.T. Barnum is putting on some exciting programs. I could do some trick riding and shooting."

"Does he have women in his show?" I asked hopefully.
"Why do you want to know?" he asked, a corner of his mouth

twitched to grin.

"If you can learn trick riding and shooting, maybe I can too." I turned to face him as I quipped.

"I know you can." He let the twitch stretch his broad mouth into a teasing smile. "It's the woman part I was questioning."

"By the time I learn to ride, I'll be a woman." Turning back to the fire, I added, "If I have to take care of these wild hooligans long, I'll dry up and blow away like the prairie."

"The prairie can be a boring place sometimes." Josh Paul's rocker creaked back and forth. "At least, we'll have fun at the jackrabbit hunt."

"What jackrabbit hunt?" I asked.

"The big jackrabbit hunt planned for the last of April." He explained, "The rabbits are eating the gardens and hay crops faster than the people or the cattle. So there's going to be a county-wide hunt." His eyes glowed and he talked faster. "Everyone will form a circle stretching all around Tulia. Then we'll round-up and trap rabbits, enclosing them in our circle. As we move inward, the circle will get smaller and smaller, chasing zillions of rabbits into cages."

"Gee-whiz," I whispered in awe. "Can girls go?"

"It should be safe enough for a shrimp." Josh Paul stood up and stretched. "Besides we'll need everybody to encircle the entire county." He took his hat off the nail by the door and placed it snugly down on his head. "I'll ask Ma if you can go with us," he said as he went out the door.

"Thank her for the stew." Half-angry with him for calling me a shrimp again, I locked the door with a slam and sat back down in the rocker, promising to get up and clean the cabin before Mama got home. Instead, I dreamed of chasing rabbits through fields of wildflowers with Josh Paul at my side. The cool breeze of summer was blowing through my hair, curly and golden in the sunlight.

Dishes clattering in the wooden tub woke me. Dawn's light squeezed through the chinks in the mud-brick walls, prying my eyelids open. I sat up with a start. Our dirt floor that had been smeared with johnnycake batter now was scraped clean and packed down hard. The tub with diapers left to soak sat drying by a small fire, and the diapers were hung on a line. As I pulled my head off a pillow that hadn't been there before I slept, a quilt slipped from my shoulders.

"Good morning, Shyanne." Mama stood at the cabinet kneading biscuit dough.

"Mama! When did you get home?" I asked in a sleepy stupor.

"It was late. Doctor Anderson had to deliver a baby out this way, and I helped him," She rolled out the fluffy white dough on a flour-sprinkled board. "Jackson heard me knocking and let me in."

"I didn't mean to fall asleep," I said, rubbing my eyes.

"You must have been very tired. Jackson said you worked hard all day and took very good care of them. He said you were the best mama—next to me, of course." She cut the biscuits out with a tin as she talked. "I suspect he gave you his saintly treatment."

The little imp, I thought to myself. "Oh, yes! He was a saint," I rolled my eyes in wonder. How could he be so mean all day and then turn to molasses when Mama got home?

"The saintly treatment," she laughed, "is Jackson's way of helping us become more patient." Mama dipped the biscuits in butter, placed them in the Dutch oven and swiveled it back over the fire almost as if her movements kept a beat to her words. "Did he jump off the windmill? Dig a tunnel deep enough to bury himself and his brothers alive? Perhaps he tied the neighbor's cat's tail in a knot? I know him!"

"Did you get the job?" I asked, afraid she didn't and afraid she did, which would mean more days for me to learn patience from Jackson.

"Yes, the Swisher County Cattleman's Association has a new cattle agent." The corners of her mouth jerked, trying to avoid the smile that twinkled in her eyes. "A broker of sorts, in charge of contracts and letters to improve beef prices." Pride strengthened her voice. She was proud, and there was no way I'd let her see my sadness about quitting school to keep the boys.

"That's wonderful, Mama." I hugged her, and she finally let the smile spread across her face.

"I wish all the ranchers felt that way." Her smile faded. "Progress is coming to Texas and these cowboys need help with the city businessmen. I'm just the lady to help them. Me and my old typing machine." She went to the cellar and pulled out the strange machine. I remembered her and Papa arguing over its place in the wagon each time we moved. Mama's eyes sparkled then just as they did now.

"I'll write letters to businesses in the North and South. I'll hire some cowboys to herd the cattle we sell to the rail station at Clarendon." She talked as she dusted the corner table near her bed. It was the table where Papa kept his homebrew. "Goodness, I know every butcher between here and Virginia." She talked so fast I couldn't keep up with her. "Then I'll write my father's friends in Washington and New York City."

I never had seen Mama so excited, except maybe when she was helping an animal give birth or singing at church. Her eyes sparkled as she continued, "We'll build a herd of cattle like my father had, prime beef–not the scrawny longhorn cattle of south Texas. The wonderful part is, I get to stay at home with my family most of the time, and you get to stay in school." She placed the little writing machine on the table and searched for paper.

"Your grandmother always said, education is your future, Shyanne. That's why she sent me to college and wouldn't let me marry your papa until I finished. Now, I have a job and I'm able to stay home with my kids, too."

I get to stay in school? It sounded too good to be true! Something would happen, I thought. Something would happen and ruin it all.

"There will be times I have to go to town or contact small ranchers who want a better price." Mama slipped a piece of paper into the typing machine. "If only one rancher will let me represent him, we can make it."

Silently, I got ready for school. Now I understood Mama's plan. It was somewhere between a real job with real money and a happy-ever-after scheme. I was disappointed. If we had to count on the men of Swisher County letting a woman help them in the cattle business, I knew it was hopeless.

※ ※ ※

April blew across the prairie and brought some much needed rain. Unfortunately the rain came on April the first. That was supposed to be the April Fool's Day picnic, and I was supposed to go with the Youngers. The next week I stayed home and kept the babies while Mama and, thank the stars, Jackson borrowed Feller and rode to some of the small ranchers in the area. She hoped they would let her sell their cattle. It was a wasted trip.

"I told you Jackson would hurt your chances," I said as Mama and I sat by the fire shelling black-eyed peas. The peas had made a young crop earlier than usual. Mama said it was God's way of taking care of us. I remembered planting seeds in boxes in a freezing barn and covering them with hay. If you asked me, God wasn't anywhere around last February, and I didn't like praising Him for the peas in April.

"It wasn't Jackson's fault I didn't get any assignments to sell cattle, and you know it." Mama grabbed a hand full of peapods from the burlap sack at our feet.

"Jackson can destroy a day before the sun comes up," I said.

"That's not true, and don't be so negative with your brother. Little boys need praise." Mama shook a peapod in my direction. "It's these men. They are so set on a woman's having her place in the home. One man had a fit when I got down from the wagon and he realized I'm 'with child,' as he put it." Mama's long, slim fingers snapped the peas with a vengeance. "How can they think we can cook, scrub, and plow when we're pregnant, but—she made her voice sound slow and arrogant, just like some of the men in Swisher County—'Lord, woman, don't try to sell cattle. That's man's work. It takes a keen mind to dicker prices.'"

Mama's mouth formed a tight line and then she continued. "Men! I shouldn't be so hard on them. For every one that thinks he's God's gift to women, there's another who is."

"I don't know why you keep trying." I wanted to sock the men who refused Mama's help. She was honest and smart. She offered to accept a much smaller percent to sell the herds than the men who were agents. Most of them were from Fort Worth or Kansas City, and they didn't know Panhandle people. The ranchers were just stupid, or they'd see what a great offer Mama was making.

"Tell 'em to jump into a rattlesnake hole," I suggested.

"Now can you see Claude Cornhurst getting his big middle in a snake hole?" Mama laughed, then grew serious again. "Do you want me to give up?" She arched her eyebrows and watched me intently. "We could go back to Grandma's."

I rolled my eyes in answer. Nothing was working out! But having nothing was better than moving to Grandma's.

I was tired, tired of waiting for tomorrow and tired of waiting for someone to let Mama sell their cattle. Since the first of April I had watched her talk to cattlemen. She had shown them letters and prices she could get for their herd, but not one would listen. Mr. Younger said, "Come next spring, I'll have a few to sell." Problem was, "next spring" never comes and I knew it.

I tried to put it out of my head. It was only a week before

the rabbit hunt, and I was afraid something would spoil it. "That rabbit hunt won't ever happen," I grumbled as I picked up another peapod. "Gloom has been hanging around our tomorrows like a pack of wolves, waiting to devour any chances of a happy time."

"That sounds like something Mr. Bulew would say," Mama picked up the last of her peas. "Predicting gloom is hard work, Shiloh." She was right! I was good and tired of it all. I concentrated on the up-and-coming great rabbit hunt's being perfect.

"You want me to read the article in the *Tulia News* again?" I asked.

"You read it word for word every day this week." As she spoke, I unfolded the worn paper and read it again.

The Great Rabbit Hunt will commence Saturday next and promises to rid the county of its rabbit infestation. According to Claude Cornhurst hundreds of dollars will be saved in crop damage. No guns allowed! Lunch will be provided.

"No guns. That's the only reason I'm letting you go," Mama said as I folded the paper clipping and tucked it back in my schoolbook.

"It will probably rain Saturday next." I dropped the peas into the empty bucket. The plink and plunk echoed my prediction of rain.

"It might not." Mama emptied her second bowl of peas into the washing vat.

"At the last minute, the Youngers probably won't be able to go," I said as I reached for another long, bumpy pod, snapped off the head, and pulled the string. "Or Josh Paul will decide he doesn't want a shrimp tagging along."

All I could do was wait, afraid the day would never come.

Chapter Eight

The Youngers picked me up long before dawn. As we traveled to meet our neighbors, I leaned back against Josh Paul's old hound dog and enjoyed the sunrise. Bright shades of pink chased the purple from the wide sky as if it were pulling the sun up by its bootstraps.

Josh Paul sharpened his knife so he'd be ready to skin what he caught. "Someone figured out there's about sixty rabbits on every section of land," he said. "How many sections in Swisher County, Pa?"

"Swisher County has about 900 square sections," Mr. Younger answered.

Josh Paul twisted his head and squinted into the rising sun. "I figured that to be 54,000 rabbits."

"That's a lot of rabbits!" I yelped.

Everyone in our part of the county waited for directions at the spot where Tule Creek formed a wide spot in the prairie. Mr. and Mrs. Younger, Josh Paul and I sat on the buckboard enjoying the sight of the crowd. Mr. Elkin stepped up on a wagon near the creekbed and shouted directions.

"Before Claude Cornhurst begins this tomfoolery, I just want to say one thing. Remember, no guns of any kind."

Then Claude Cornhurst climbed up beside him. His rounded belly made it difficult for him to balance, but he snatched off his weathered hat and smiled like the sun was a spotlight and the old wagon a great stage. "Start at the county line close to your land and don't spread out too far. Each person is to have a club. Chase the rabbits in, keeping your circle as tight as possible. Club 'em when you can and drop 'em down in these sacks." He waved a burlap sack over his head. "Meet in the center of town for lunch."

Everyone whooped and hollered, then took off in a cloud of dust. Mr. Younger strolled back to the wagon, laughing and shaking his head.

"You still think this is foolish?" Mrs. Younger asked.

"Foolish, yes," he chuckled. "But it's entertaining."

As we headed for the county line, I leaned toward Josh Paul and asked in a whisper, "Why does your pa think this is foolish?"

"D.O.G. here is as fast a dog as I've ever seen," he said scratching his mutt's tattered ear. "He huffs and puffs trying to catch those long-legged jackrabbits." D.O.G., whose name spelled out his pedigree—nothing fancy, just plain dog—pawed at Josh Paul's hand to get him to continue petting him.

I thought about the time I had tried to chase a rabbit, and I didn't see how it would work, either. "Why didn't your pa tell Mr. Elkin?" I asked with sensible female logic.

"Mr. Elkin knows." He answered in a man's logic, which never makes sense when they're discussing hunting, fishing or bragging. "Claude Cornhurst and some of the other men really believe it'll rid us of the varmints."

We had fifteen miles to drive out before we turned to start back. The Love family, the Lemmons and the Mayfields all joined us in a line. It was good they all had so many kids, because the land stretched as far as you could see. There were plenty of gaps in the line of people, much like there were in Mr. Cornhurst's plan. Mrs. Younger stayed in the wagon.

"I'm driving the wagon. There's no sense in my walking myself to death for Cornhurst's folly," Mrs. Younger stated firmly as she picked up the reins. "We'll need the wagon to get home later and to carry the big lunch basket in case we don't make it to the cages."

"Spread out, Shrimp." Josh Paul said as he moved about ten yards away from me.

We walked only a few feet, when long, twitching ears popped up from a patch of prairie grass. Jackrabbits raced across an open area until they reached another stand of tall grass and hid. I couldn't believe how easy it was, like herding cattle.

We stalked on about a mile, and then the easy part was over. The four or five rabbits I had prodded, turned and scampered back. I looked at Josh Paul for help. He had his hands full with the same problem. Even though the gap separating us had shrunk, the pesky little devils scurried past. A big one veered away from me and darted toward Josh Paul.

"Get him!" I yelled.

Josh Paul lunged for the rabbit in a valiant display. He missed and landed in a cactus bed.

"I'll be dad-burned!" He cursed as he rolled over and pulled a long, cactus spine out of his trousers. Three rabbits headed my direction. "Look out!" he called.

The first one zigged to the left just out of my reach. The second zagged to the right, jumping over my long stick. And the third ran right through my legs, toppling me over in a heap.

Josh Paul's laughter blended with the shouts and laughter of the other hunters. Once, I thought I heard the jackrabbits chuckle. We must have looked pretty silly.

For the next couple of hours, the scene was repeated up and down our line of fearless hunters. Rabbits would play our game until they were about a mile from their homes and then they would tire of us. They raced by, leaving us sprawled in a heap on the prairie. By noon we gave up and found a spot to enjoy Mrs. Younger's lunch.

"No sense in wasting a day on this folderol." Mrs. Younger stopped picking up the lunch fixings long enough to shake a spoon at her husband. "Jess Younger, if you have time to chase rabbits that don't intend to be caught, then you have time to take me to the store. I saw a bolt of blue material at Cantrells' and I need a new dress."

"I hate not being around to see old Claude's face." Mr. Younger put his hat on and stood, stretching his six-foot frame toward the cloudless sky. "However, I'd hate more not seeing you in that pretty blue dress," he added, giving his wife a hug.

"Jess, the kids!" She tried to sound angry with him, but it was clear that she loved his affection. I thought about Papa, and wondered if he was still alive.

When we got near the schoolhouse, Josh Paul asked his pa to stop. "I need my reader," he explained.

I knew there had to be another reason he wanted to stop. He had that reader memorized and only read out of it to help the smaller kids. He had read all of Miss Gibson's books many times over, too.

Mr. Younger reined the horses to a stop. "Don't be long."

"Come help me, Shyanne." Josh Paul took my hand and pulled me off the wagon, then turned to his pa. "You can go on to the store, sir." He was up to something, for sure. When we got near the school, he stopped dead in his tracks at the corner of the building. The shock on his face was exaggerated as he pointed at the tree.

"Why look at Miss Gibson's tree!" he said, running up to it. "It's as green as winter wheat."

It was green and much thinner. I reached out and touched it, expecting the paint covered needles to fall off in my hand. They were soft.

"There it is, Shyanne, your miracle!" Josh Paul announced proudly.

"And you're a crawdad's cousin," I answered back. "That's not Miss Gibson's tree."

"Whose tree could it be?" he argued. The much too innocent look on his face revealed he had been up to something.

"I don't care whose it is. I know it's not the fat little tree you cut for Shenandoah."

He dug in the dirt with the toe of his boot. "I agree it's thinner, but it had to shed its needles to stimulate its roots."

I walked past the tree and headed for the door with a smirk on my face. "Oh, it shed them all right." It was a good story, typical of Josh Paul's imagination. He side-stepped the truth like a politician. The fact was clear to me he had thrown away the dead tree and replaced it with a new one. This tree came in on his uncle's supply wagon straight from Colorado, as sure as coyotes howl.

"I told you a miracle would come along and it has. You just can't admit when you're wrong," he said as I laughed.

Later that night, the day's adventure flashed through my mind like picture tintypes. I had to smile. Josh Paul had gone to so much trouble to get a tree and try to convince me that a miracle had happened. I couldn't refuse him a little pleasure. From now on, I'd pretend to believe in his miracle tree.

Chapter Nine

In the wee hours of May first, rain pelted our sod roof. Rain again! I groaned. Rain meant the spring festival, including the maypole dance, would be cancelled. I had been nominated to be May Queen. Prissy was also nominated, so it was pretty certain I wouldn't win. If Shenandoah were alive, she'd be the queen. I had little chance, if any. However, a small dream hid deep in my heart: I dreamed Josh Paul would crown me as queen, even though he didn't choose the queen. The people of the community voted by giving pennies to the school building fund. Somehow I felt if he crowned me it would prove to Priscilla and Adele that he was my beau. Like Cinderella and Prince Charming, our names would be forever intertwined.

"Cow manure," I moaned into my pillow. "Lovesick, cow manure!"

By noon the ornery Texas weather had become a pussy cat, purring with soft sunshine and gentle breezes. Mama let the hem down in my Sunday dress and added a row of lace trying to make it look like a dress fit for a May Queen. My brown shoes poked their scuffed toes out underneath, but I smiled and told Mama how nice it looked. It didn't matter that Prissy would have a brand new one. I wouldn't win, but I hoped that Josh Paul had been the one to nominate me. If I knew he thought of me as a queen, or a young woman, or anything but a shrimp, I would feel like a winner. Mama tugged on my hem to smooth it down. Then she took a double knot and broke the thread.

"You can't hide scuffed-toed shoes under lace!" Mama said with a sigh.

"No, you can't." I agreed, feeling like I was the scuffed-toe shoes trying to hide as a May Queen.

"Maybe in the fall . . ." Mama started to say more, then stood up and put away her needle and thread. Her eyes were tired. She hadn't mentioned Papa in a long time. "This baby seems to be sitting up higher." She took a deep breath. "Makes it a might harder to breathe."

Mama did seem to be looking fuller in the tummy. All we needed were twins!

I sat on my bed and brushed my hair all afternoon, hoping it would shine.

"Shyanne's hair's gonna fall out if she don't stop brushing it," Augusta said.

"Then she'll be bald!" Jackson giggled.

"Get out of my room," I yelled.

"We are." Augusta looked at his feet and then at me. He and Jackson stood near the eating table, well into the living area of our dugout. The cubbyhole I called a room grew smaller each day. It felt more like a stage, where every part of my life was on view for my little brothers' entertainment. Angry, I jerked shut the curtains that Mama had hung in front of my bed.

"Boys," Mama called softly, "go out and gather the eggs."

🌹 🌹 🌹

By the time the Youngers came to take us to town, Mama had her hair pinned up and was looking as beautiful as ever. I got in the back with Josh Paul and the boys. It could have been a wonderful ride into the late afternoon sun if Jackson hadn't been born with a musical ear.

"Listen, Josh Paul," Jackson kept pulling on Josh Paul's arm. "Listen to me play "Yankee Doodle."

"Jackson," I said under my breath. "Can't you see we're talking!"

"Don't you wanna hear me, Josh Paul?" He pushed in

between the two of us.

"No! He doesn't." I tried to move him back to where his brothers sat at the front of the wagon bed.

"Sure, Jackson." Josh Paul ruffled Jackson's hair. "Are you going to hum?"

"No. I play it under my arm," Jackson bragged.

"Don't you do it!" I threatened Jackson with my hand.

"What?" Josh Paul laughed. "Can you really?"

"No!" I grabbed Jackson before he could slip his hand into his shirt and start making obnoxious noises.

"Wait, Shrimp." Josh Paul's words felt like a slap in the face. "I've got to hear talent like this!"

Jackson proceeded to cup one hand over his arm pit and press his arm against his side. As the air expelled around his hand he moved it to form different pitches until the crude tune of "Yankee Doodle" could be heard in the warm, still night.

I groaned. Augusta applauded and Josh Paul laughed. Finally, Mama made Jackson stop, but Josh Paul had called me a shrimp. Again!

All week we had worked getting the school ready for the spring festival. Now the decorations hung in rows around the schoolroom and gave it a special atmosphere. Miss Gibson welcomed the parents. Then Josh Paul introduced the students who had memory work. Abigail and her large gray cat recited, "Keeping School in Play."

"Come, Kitty dear, I'll tell you what
We'll do this rainy day;"

Abigail held her tabby around its fluffy middle. The kitty twitched its ears and looked bored.

"Just you and I, all by ourselves,
At keeping school, will play.
The teacher, Kitty, I will be;
And you shall be the class;
You must close attention give,

81

If you expect to pass."

Abigail's round face crunched up at the kitty, and then her brown eyes would grow large and round. I almost liked her until she finished her poem. Then she flipped her blond curls and stuck her nose up just like Prissy. She walked past the audience and threw her cat out the door like it was a bother and she was a royal princess.

Prissy gave a syrupy rendition of "Couldn't Do Without Bessie," as though anyone who knew her would believe that she'd dust and scrub to help her ailing mama. Everyone applauded. I knew she had nothing in common with kind Bessie in the poem.

Tom Spencer recited "The Charge of the Light Brigade." As he yelled "rode" his eyes widened with wild excitement, and with each "brave" he sniffed and wiped his nose on his sleeve.

The children's portion of the program drew to an end, and we circled the maypole outside. The sun was riding near the horizon, casting pink and purple rays across the broad sky. Miss Gibson handed each child one of the colorful ribbons of cloth that dangled from the flag pole. We each took the ribbon in the hand nearest the pole and stepped out until each streamer was straight. Then we moved in a colored pinwheel under the pole.

Mr. Younger played his fiddle, and Mr. Love played his guitar. Every other person in the Maypole walked clockwise. The other half walked counter-clockwise. Over and under, over and under we walked weaving the ribbons in a rainbow around the pole. Not wanting anything to go wrong, I paid close attention to my movements. Tom Spencer kept trying to go over my ribbon when he was suppose to go under. When the ribbons were wrapped tightly around the pole, we reversed and unwound until we stood where we had begun. Each child reached out and took their mama's or papa's hand. Then the adults took their turn.

"I can't do this," Mama argued as I offered her the ribbon.

"You have to." I thrust the ribbon into her hand and took Shawnee. "Have fun!"

Mama laughed and tapped her toe as the music began. She moved easily through the crowd. Watching her, I realized how beautiful she must have been before hard times aged her. Her eyes laughed as she ducked to go under the ribbon in front of her.

"I don't think anyone who is in a family way should be allowed to participate." Prissy was at my elbow. "Aren't you embarrassed?"

"At what?" I asked.

"At your mother making a fool of herself." Prissy rolled her eyes in disgust. "Not only is she trying to be a man in the cattle business, now she's practically dancing before a crowd."

"This isn't dancing." I felt my cheeks grow hot with anger.

"Oh, it might as well be. They just don't call it dancing because all the Methodists and Baptists think dancing is sinful. I'm glad my parents are Presbyterian. I can do anything I want and call it predestination."

"I guess that explains why you are so stupid." Shifting Shawnee to a new position on my shoulder I tried to move away from Prissy.

"It explains why I'm going to be crowned May Queen." She grabbed my arm and turned me toward her. A smirk twisted her lips. "It is the same reason my daddy is a Mason and yours is gone. It's the reason my mother was chosen for the Eastern Star and your mother wasn't." She pressed my arm with one fat finger to emphasize each word. Predestination. "That, my sad little friend, is why I'll be crowned May Queen. And you-know-who is going to crown me." She laughed and walked away.

I wanted to sit Shawnee down in the dirt and hit Prissy. I'd grab her by the ears like a cow, kick her legs out from under her and twist her neck until she flopped down on her side and cried "Calf rope!"

The music stopped and Mama drew my thoughts away

from Prissy. Josh Paul was on the schoolhouse steps announcing the names of the two nominees for May Queen.

". . . and Shiloh Jones." He seemed to choke on my real name. I guess he had never said it before. Prissy, dressed in a blue flowered dress, was already on the step beside him. I went to the other side as Josh Paul read Prissy's accomplishments.

"Priscilla Babcock has made the highest marks in her class for six years. She does charity work with her mother and has ten pen pals. She has received two perfect attendance pens and three memory pens in Sunday School. She is kindhearted and loved by her classmates." Josh Paul almost laughed as he read the last comment.

Then he stammered around at my lack of accomplishments. I wished I had taken more care in writing them out.

"Shiloh is an honest person. She helps Miss Gibson each day after school." He turned the paper over and looked for more accomplishments. Then he crumpled it at his side and made up his own. "Shiloh Jones is a wonderful daughter and sister. She works night and day helping her ma raise her five little brothers."

I cringed in humiliation. Did he have to make it sound like we were poor and had too many kids? Even if it was true, it wasn't something I wanted to brag about.

"She knows all her nine multiplication tables." He said proudly.

I wanted to slip through the cracks in the porch. Everyone else in sixth grade knew all their tables. My eyes rolled to the back of my head. This had to be what it felt like to die.

"She can out-fish, out-run and out-climb any boy in the county." He stated proudly. "Except me, of course."

I shook my head. At least he finally said something that made me proud. The only reason I hadn't beaten him was because I was too smart to try. Tears stung my eyes, but I laughed along with everyone else.

"Now, the girl you have chosen as your May Queen is . . . ."

He took another paper from Miss Gibson and unfolded it. He looked at me like Shawnee does before he throws up. "Priscilla Babcock."

Everyone clapped and Prissy nodded a queen's blessing to her royal subjects. I clapped wildly, but I wanted to run. I hated her for being the daughter of an Eastern Star, for being predestined, but most of all for saying mean things about Mama.

The hardest part of the entire evening was pretending it didn't matter. I pretended I didn't care about being queen, and really I didn't, but I didn't like Josh Paul and Prissy starting the Old Dan Tucker game. Josh Paul didn't seem too thrilled about it either. He stood as long as he could without holding her hand. They walked through the lines of players, and he smiled at everyone but Prissy.

Even Miss Gibson was playing, and the cowboy beside her seemed more interested in her than in the game. I wanted to tell him he was grazing in the wrong pasture. Miss Gibson had her head set on a career, not taking care of a scrawny cowboy.

"I'm taking Shawnee and Russell to the wagon," I told Mama.

"Don't you want to play?" she asked.

"No, it's just dancing without the good part, the music," I explained. "Besides, I have a headache."

"Maybe the Youngers will want to leave soon." Mama felt my brow and tugged on my ear. It was her special signal to remind me that she loved me. I took Shawnee and Russell by their hands, and I walked away from the party, the laughter and my one small dream.

We got up into the wagon and spread one of the quilts Mrs. Younger brought for us. Shawnee snuggled up and quickly went to sleep. Russell wriggled and wriggled until I sang to him. He finally slept, and then I cried. When the Youngers, Mama and the boys came to the wagon, I pretended to be asleep.

85

Chapter Ten

May ended. School was out. Summertime is lonely on the prairie, especially when you're used to having your sister as your best friend. My heavy loneliness for Shenandoah kept pulling me down.

In July, the heat became unbearable. Our dugout, half buried in the dirt, was usually cool at night, but by the last of July, it was ember-hot and desert-dry. Not a breath of wind could find my cubbyhole. I dragged my mattress out of the dugout and put it on the cellar door.

"Shyanne, what are you doing?" Mama called to me from the porch.

"My bed is hotter than a potato in a bed of red coals!" I yelled back.

"Be careful, you know the snakes love that cellar in the summertime. Wolves and mountain lions have been roaming out of the canyons lately."

Ignoring her, I lay on my back looking at the sky. It was so crowded with stars, another one couldn't find a place to wink if it wanted to. Some blinked, others glowed a steady shade of pink. All were so close, I could almost touch them.

A nearby howl startled me. "Just a coyote," I assured myself. An old hoot owl flew out of the barn. And I thought I heard the scream of a mountain lion floating across the prairie. While I explained that away as the creaking of the windmill, I heard the clattering sound of a snake's rattlers. Nothing else made that spine-tingling rattle. I froze.

The vegetables I had eaten for supper rose in my throat

with fear close behind. My jaw ached from being clenched tight. The rattling stopped. Fearing it would strike, praying it would leave, I shut my eyes and waited. A slithering sound rustled in dry grass, assuring me the reptile was gone. I took a deep breath, my first in several minutes. Then I grabbed my mattress and ran back to my hot cubby hole. It had been small and cramped for Shenandoah and me. Now, it was empty but safe.

🌹 🌹 🌹

In the pre-dawn hours I woke up with a start. I had been dreaming that I was in a small, dark place, and I couldn't breathe. Something clammy and cold touched my face. I sat up quickly.

"Shenandoah?" I whispered, reaching out to my sister's side of the bed. She had always comforted me when I had bad dreams. "Shenandoah, I had a terrible dream," I whispered.

When my hand touched nothing but an empty bed, I remembered. Shenandoah wasn't there any more. How could you have forgotten? I chided myself. How could you ever forget? She's dead, and you can never tell her you love her.

Fumbling to light the oil lamp, I discovered a slimy salamander had dropped from the sod wall and fallen on my face.

"Dang your hide! You scared me to death," I yelled as I jerked the bedclothes off my bed.

"Shyanne!" Mama warned. "Where did you pick up such language?"

I wanted to tell her I got it from Papa and that I had cleaned it up considerably, but I knew it was best to apologize.

"I'm sorry, Mama. An old salamander fell out of the wall and scared me to death."

"Why don't you come crawl in beside me for the rest of the night?" she invited.

As I lay beside her, I wondered if she had heard me cry for Shenandoah. She must miss her too—and Papa.

🌹 🌹 🌹

I woke the next morning with a heavy weight on my chest. Hot air puffed against my face and the smell of maple syrup filled my nostrils. The events of the long night before came back to me—the snake, the salamander and taking refuge in Mama's bed like a scared rabbit. Slowly, I woke up. Two enormous brown eyes over a pug nose seriously investigated my nose and mouth.

"S'yann, you waked up!" Murfrees straddled my waist and lay on my chest, his nose inches from mine. "Mama said, mustn't wake up S'yann! Me didn't!"

"You didn't?" I groaned.

"Nope!" he answered proudly. His sticky fingers patted my cheeks and examined my lips. The taste of syrup marked their tracks as his fingers insisted on parting my lips and trying to pry open my teeth.

"Don't, Murfrees!" I mumbled holding my lips together.

"I wanna see that funny thing in you' mouth." He pushed against my teeth until I had to turn my head away.

"What funny thing?" I asked through clenched teeth.

"That thing that wiggles when you sound like this 'sng-woor!'" He snorted like a baby pig at feeding time.

"Sngwoor! Sngwoor, yourself!" I mimicked as I pushed him off my chest and tickled his chubby chin until laughter rumbled out of him. Getting out of Mama's bed, I added, "I'll have you know, I don't snore."

"Sngwoor! Sngwoor!" Murfrees teased.

I grabbed at him, but he ran, bouncing giggles out with each step. After I made Mama's bed, I chased him and scooped him up into my arms. Then we searched for the rest of the wild tribe. The other four boys were in the leanto where Mama was doing my chores.

"I'm sorry I overslept," I said, sitting Murfrees down to play with his brothers. Augusta and Jackson swung on the chicken-roost gate, and Russell and Shawnee shared a washtub lined with a quilt.

"Good morning, honey." Mama spread fresh hay across Sally's stall. Dust particles danced in the sunlight beaming through the large opening and shimmered around Mama's head like a halo. "Did you get enough sleep?" she asked.

"Probably more than you did," I answered as I walked up the three steps to the chicken roost and added new hay to their nest.

"Well, I didn't have salamanders visiting me in the middle of the night." She raised her voice so its soft tone would reach me in the chicken roost.

When I came down she continued, "It's ridiculous for you to put up with those pesky things crawling through the sod. We'll line the walls behind your bed with cedar posts. When your Papa comes back, it will be a while before he starts building the real house he promised."

I wanted to yell at her to stop dreaming, that Papa was never coming home, but I couldn't. She hung on to her last strands of hope like Shenandoah had hung on to life.

"You're growing into a young woman," she continued. "Soon, you'll need more privacy."

I looked down at my shapeless form and asked, "Where am I growing? I can't see it."

"Some people grow faster on the outside, than on the inside. You're lucky. You're growing on the inside first. It's easier that way." Mama's words didn't make sense to me, but they made me feel better.

She picked up Shawnee and placed him on her hip. Her dress clung to her growing figure. As she plucked bits of hay from his blond curls, I worried about what the future would bring for the new baby. Mama kept talking.

"I'll ask Mr. Younger if you can go with them to the canyon to cut some posts."

Excitement must have shown on my face. A trip to the Palo

Duro with Josh Paul! I'd cut posts or anything else to get to go.

"Jackson can help you carry them." Mama's words popped my bubble of excitement.

"Jackson? Help?" I couldn't believe she would use those two words in the same sentence. "Jackson won't be any help. We'll need help if he goes!" I argued. "Believe me!"

Mama took Russell's hand and pulled him out of the wash tub. "Augusta has a cough, besides Jackson is almost as big and he needs to do his share," she said in her I-don't-want-any-argument voice. "Lord knows, you and I have more work than we can do. Jackson is smart and good with his hands. He'll help you!"

The memory of Jackson locking me out of the dugout flashed through my brain. "He's good with his hands all right," I grumbled.

When we came out of the lean-to, a man on horseback rode toward us.

"Frau Jones?" The stranger wore a flat-topped hat and spoke with a heavy accent.

"Yes," Mama answered. "I'm Mrs. Jones."

"My name is Hans Schleicher. I have a ranch in Castro County. Someone says you are a cattle agent. You get good prices."

"Please step down, Mr. Schleicher." Mama motioned toward the babies, and I hurried them in the dugout and up the loft. Jackson darted toward the stranger, but I grabbed his hand. Mama had business and needed an office instead of a dugout full of noisy boys. I kept them quiet with a promise of cookies. Every once in a while I could hear Mama's conversation.

"Are you sure you want to trust a woman, Mr. Schleicher?" Mama asked.

"I trust one everyday, Frau Jones. My wife is also my business partner." The raspy sounds of the German's voice made it hard to understand. "I know how it is for you. In this country, people who speak a different language understand being treated unfairly. It's easier for me to trust one who also fights prejudice."

"Mr. Schleicher, I appreciate your trust. I'll mail the prices to you in a few days."

"Danke, Frau Jones."

The stranger left. After a moment I let the boys go downstairs, I expected to hear Mama whoop and howl for joy. But she didn't. She just smiled.

Chapter Eleven

Mr. Younger and Josh Paul picked Jackson and me up early the next Saturday morning, long before sun-up, and traveled to the canyon's rim. The Palo Duro Canyon stretched beneath us like a large gaping mouth, waiting to devour anyone who lost their footing on its high rim. A trail twisted down to the Prairie Dog Fork of the Red River where it snaked across the canyon floor. Every month or so rains would wash down the canyon rim and offer a brief drink to the mesquite and scrub cedars that clung to its banks.

"Wow!" Jackson stood up in the wagon and exclaimed loudly, "It's a big hole!"

"Not so big." Josh Paul stretched his legs into the space where Jackson had been sitting. "Arizona has one that's bigger."

"Bigger than Texas?" Jackson asked in disbelief. "Papa says that nothing's bigger or better than Texas!"

"Then we moved to Texas and found out the only things bigger are the grasshoppers." I smirked, remembering how Papa had bragged. "And the only thing better is the dust storms! I've yet to see anything in Texas that was bigger or better than the other states where we've lived."

"Maybe the hearts of the people," Mr. Younger said as he kept a tight rein on the horses and maneuvered them down the trail.

I thought for a moment and then asked, "But didn't the people move to Texas from some other place?"

"Yep, I guess they did, little miss." Mr. Younger chuckled.

"Little miss" sounded like a compliment when he said it.

It made me feel grown-up and dainty, instead of like a small, dumb kid.

"The Palo Duro's mighty big if you haven't seen anything else. Isn't it, Jackson?" Mr. Younger asked over his shoulder, keeping a sharp eye on the trail.

"The most amazing part is, it takes you by surprise," Josh Paul added as he grabbed Jackson's suspenders to keep him from toppling out of the wagon. "Everything's so flat all around that you don't see the canyon coming."

"Looks like some monster took a big bite of the ground." Jackson settled back down on Josh Paul's knee and looked at him in hero worship.

"A long time ago when the settlers first came to the plains, some of them drove right off into the canyon," Josh Paul said.

"They did not!" I argued.

"Yes, they did," he answered with a lift of his chin.

"That's right, Shyanne," Mr. Younger agreed as he flicked the reins to encourage Feller and their new mare, Lady, down the path into the canyon. "Late in the evening or sometimes in broad daylight, if a settler snoozed or day-dreamed his team would be over the edge before he knew the canyon was there."

"Over the edge and all the way down!" Josh Paul teasingly pushed Jackson to the edge of the wagon and threatened to toss him over.

"No! Help, Sister!" Jackson yelled between laughter and squeals.

"You better be good today, or I'll let him throw you over," I warned, adding a sound pat to his backside.

Mr. Younger pulled the wagon up near a stand of small cedars and unhitched the horses. Josh Paul and I tied them to a tree. Sunshine striped the canyon floor, marking the jagged edge of its rim. I had only been to the Palo Duro a few times and was almost as excited as Jackson. On most of those times we had come for the same reason we came today—to cut cedar posts. I knew that by noon we'd be hot and exhausted.

🌹 🌹 🌹

I was right. By noon, my back felt as crooked as some of the posts. Josh Paul and Mr. Younger cut. Jackson helped me carry the posts to the wagon. For a soon-to-be five-year-old, he worked hard, as hard as the rest of us.

"Son," Mr. Younger took off his hat and wiped his forehead with the back of his sleeve, "get that basket your ma packed and let's see if her chicken is as good as I remember."

"It's pretty hot here, Pa. Maybe we should take Feller and Lady on down to the creek for a nice cool drink," Josh Paul suggested. There was a big grin on his face.

"You think the horses need to cool off?" Mr. Younger gave a laugh and then turned to me. "Shyanne, do you think Feller and Lady could use a cooling off in the creek?"

Josh Paul looked at me and winked. Then I understood their game. "Yes, sir, I do. Cooling off is important for a horse."

"Well, get them hitched up and let's go." Mr. Younger ordered.

We worked fast, only stopping to wipe the sweat out of our eyes. We had both horses hitched and were in the wagon before Mr. Younger could take off his gloves and clean off his ax.

The team drove us deeper into the canyon and stopped near the stream. As promised, Josh Paul unhitched Feller and Lady, and we led them to the water. At the edge of the creek, Josh Paul pulled off his shoes and splashed in faster than the prairie dogs scurried into their holes. I tucked my skirt up into the waist band of my apron in pants-like fashion and tugged off Jackson's oversized boots and socks before removing my own. Jackson joined Josh Paul without being asked.

"Here I come!" He yelled as he catapulted into Josh Paul's arms.

"Watch out for holes!" I yelled. The stream was only knee

deep on Josh Paul, but I didn't want to take any chances on losing Jackson.

The mud-red water felt cool on my hot dusty feet. As I closed my eyes the stream seem to cool me all over.

"Watch out!" Josh Paul yelled. "Something has my feet!" His eyes got big and he waved his arms like he was losing his balance. "Oh no!" he screamed as he fell into the water, thrashed and carried on.

With a worried expression, Jackson ran to me and jumped into my arms. I would have headed out of the water if I didn't know Josh Paul's crazy ways.

Sure enough, he stopped his thrashing suddenly and looked up with a sheepish grin. "Gee, I hate getting wet all over."

"Oh, no!" I yelled, "it has me too." Before I could teeter and fall, Jackson was laughing. He slipped down out of my arms and plopped into the stream.

"Help! Something has me!" he shouted. Only his round face stayed out of the water, floating like a johnnycake—a round one. How could he be so ornery and so delightful?

🌹 🌹 🌹

After we ate Mrs. Younger's fried chicken, Mr. Younger stretched his long arms over his head, making himself look even taller. "Those horses need a little nap, don't you think, Shyanne," he asked me with a wink.

"They do look mighty tired." I winked back.

"I think I'll stretch out under the wagon and let them rest," he added.

"Yes, sir. That Feller's getting old!" Josh Paul teased.

"Well, so will you some day." Mr. Younger swatted him playfully with his hat. "Then we'll see who takes a nap first."

"I'll put the lunch away," I offered. "Jackson, you go rest."

"I'm not tired." He formed his mouth into the tight line I

had learned to dread. "I want Josh Paul to take me up on that big hill." He pointed to the sharp incline on the west side of the canyon wall. "It looks like a big cellar door and I wanna slide down it."

"It does look like a slide, don't it." Mr. Younger stopped and surveyed it, then warned, "I don't think anyone but the devil could slide down it. Wouldn't bother him. His backside is already hotter than fire." He ambled to the wagon and relaxed in its shade.

"Go stretch out beside Mr. Younger, Jackson," I said, putting on my sternest face.

He stared at me and then squinted his eyes like he was trying to make me disappear. Slowly, he joined Mr. Younger. I felt grown up and powerful to have made him mind me without a fight.

Josh Paul and I straightened up the lunch basket and tied the horses so they could graze on the grass growing on the edge of the creek.

When we got back to the wagon, Jackson was gone. My heart sank to my stomach, while my eyes immediately searched the steep wall.

"Jackson!" I screamed as I spotted him almost at the top.

Josh Paul ran after him, and I followed quickly.

"Jackson! Come down!" I demanded. A little ways up the hill my feet turned to lead and my lungs ached for air.

Above me, Josh Paul had slowed too. "Wait for me, Jackson," he pleaded.

"Jackson!" I gasped. My words were useless. In the wink of an eye, he was over the edge. At first on his backside, then he lost control, spun to his side and began to tumble.

"Help!" His little voice sounded terrified.

Josh Paul carefully sidestepped out on to the incline in an attempt to stop the small form hurtling down the canyon wall. Jackson whizzed past in a blur of rocks and dirt, then dropped in a twisted heap on the clay floor below.

Without breathing, I watched. His small frame lay motionless. All I could think of was telling Mama I had failed her once more.

Josh Paul slid down the incline and rushed to Jackson's side, but I stood frozen to the side of the cliff. I couldn't go home. I couldn't live. Through my tears, I saw Mr. Younger carefully turn Jackson over. Josh Paul ran to the creek and soaked his handkerchief, then ran back.

I sank to the ground and dropped my forehead to my knees and cried—cried for every misery of my miserable life.

"Sister!" Jackson's voice called through the fog of my misery. "Sister, I'm not hurt."

Believing the call to be an angel's voice, praying that it wasn't, I looked. "Jackson?" I whispered. "Jackson, are you alive?"

"He's alive alright!" Josh Paul called up to me. "He wants to do it again."

"Jackson, I'm gonna tan your hide and string it on barbed wire!" I threatened. Tears washed down my hot cheeks. Before I reached the bottom, I wiped them away and wore my angriest face.

Jackson was, as usual, two steps ahead of me. He sat on the wagon in between Josh Paul and Mr. Younger, looking like an angel.

As we traveled home, one minute I was thanking God Jackson was alive and the next minute, I was thinking of ways to kill him.

Chapter Twelve

"Heroes," I shrugged. "Why are they always men?"

Miss Gibson laughed softly as we applauded the end of Mr. J.H. Settle's speech.

Each July 17th the Swisher County Reunion Celebration was held at Battle Ground Canyon where General Ranald S. Mackenzie defeated a band of Indians. Tule Creek was crystal clear in this southern section of the canyon, or at least would be until the kids got in and started playing. Trees made it a perfect place for a picnic. Every year there were more and more people at the county's birthday celebration.

"Heroes?" Miss Gibson looked at me. I could tell she was thinking of how to answer my question. "Not all heroes are men. There's Dorothea Dix and Clara Barton. They were heroes," she said as she smoothed her hair back under her straw hat. A blue ribbon, matching the short-sleeve dress she wore, was tied at the side of the hat.

"Naw!" I muttered. "Women like Clara Barton only took care of the sick and fed people. I mean a real hero, that shoots the bad guys!" I let my gaze wander over the crowd as I talked. "Every year we have the reunion picnic, and the politicians talk about war heroes—Austin, Houston, Mackenzie. Never Mrs. Austin, Mrs. Houston, or Mrs. Mackenzie. No one mentions the number of bandages some nurses rolled."

"I bet the soldiers who are alive because of those bandages mention the nurses." Miss Gibson smiled as she looked around.

"Why can't the women go to war and the men stay home and cook and clean?" I asked, thinking mostly of Jackson and other four-year-old tornadoes.

"Women tend to want to talk problems out." Miss Gibson tried to explain, "while men act first and seldom talk. Think about it a minute. If there were a gang of desperados charging the county and women were defending the homes, we'd offer the villains dinner and ask about their families. Now if these were just misunderstood men, acting naughty, we'd be safe enough. We might even help them become law-abiding citizens." Miss Gibson's eyes moved around the picnic area. "But what if those desperados were really evil? They would have our throats cut and be off with our children before we said grace."

"Not me!" I bragged. "I'd shoot better than Crockett or Goodnight if Papa would have ever let me touch the shotgun."

"Well, half the stories men tell about shooting and killing are more fiction that fact, Shiloh. Charles Goodnight wrote that few men were killed on the Plains after the Indian Wars."

"But to hear the stories some of the old-timers tell, there were bank robbers and desperados on every trail." I bit my lip and tried to figure it out. "I still want to hear about women heroes."

"Is this a picnic or a history lesson?" She laughed as she straightened her hat and started walking toward the speakers stand. "Why don't you write a report about it?"

Oh, cow manure! I thought to myself. When would I learn to stop asking questions. I asked out loud, "Is that an assignment?"

"No, just a suggestion." She smiled.

I breathed a sigh of relief.

"Look, Shiloh." She pointed toward the creek. "The younger children look bored. Why don't you organize a game?"

"Thanks, Miss Gibson," I said, glad to be out of doing a report. She walked off, then turned to study a quilt to be raffled. Soon a cowboy came toward her. He took off his hat. Miss Gibson lit up like a moonbeam. There was a marriage proposal in his smile and a "yes" in hers. I didn't want to lose her as our teacher. She was the best.

"Shyanne!" Josh Paul called me. I searched the crowd, but I couldn't see him.

"Up here, Shrimp." He stood on a hill halfway up the canyon wall, beside the old cannon. He wore a green shirt and a cocky grin. I walked toward him, instead of running like I would have done if he hadn't called me Shrimp.

"What have you been doing?" he asked.

"Miss Gibson and I were having an in-tel-lectual conversation about the stupidity of men," I answered and tried to jump up on the cannon's barrel. My dress got in the way so I tried again. This time I was successful. Josh Paul looked up at me and squinted one eye.

"The stupidity of men? Is that a fact?" He gave me a serious look. "Men, not women or people, but men are the stupid ones?"

"Fact!" I answered. "Especially those that call a grown girl a shrimp."

"You're right." Josh Paul nodded his head. "But I think a grown girl who sits on a cannon barrel that's about to be fired, isn't too smart." He laughed and pointed behind me.

I looked around in time to see Mr. Settle and the sheriff lighting the torch they would use to ignite the cannon. I jumped off faster than a cannon ball could fly through the air. A ripping sound followed me.

"What was that?" Josh Paul asked.

Feeling behind me, I discovered my dress and my bloomers torn clear through to bare skin.

"Come on," Josh Paul pulled me away from the cannon. I tried to hold the rip closed as we ran a safe distance. We plugged our ears and I scooted up to the canyon wall to hide my backside.

The mayor shouted a few words. Then the sheriff lit the

fuse. The old cannon blasted and rang in my ears for several minutes.

"Wow! That was great!" Josh Paul exclaimed.

"Best yet." I said, remembering last year. "Now what am I going to do with a torn dress and drawers?"

"Let's see," he said.

"No, sir!" I answered, backing closer to the wall.

"Is it that bad?" he grinned.

"I should have known something would happen to ruin my good time," I said. "Nothing ever works out."

"Just cover it up." He shrugged and started to walk down the hill.

"With what?" I asked.

"I don't know. Use your bonnet." He walked off and joined the kids near the creek. I watched him ignore Prissy and say "hey" to the boys. When he began talking to two girls from Union Hill, I took my bonnet off and tied it around my dress. I wasn't about to miss the picnic.

I ran to join the group as they marked the boundary for blindman's buff. Part of the play area was in the creek and part was near low hanging cedars. It would be fun.

Tom Spencer was "It." Josh Paul was tying a blindfold around his eyes and asking him the riddle.

"Now, Buff!" Josh Paul turned Tom around and around, "How many horses does your father have?"

"Three," Tom answered. By this time most people would be a little goofy from spinning, but Tom acted goofy all the time, so it was difficult to tell if he had been spun long enough.

"What color are they?" I yelled the signal for him to be spun again as I came into the playing area.

"Black, white and gray," he responded as Josh Paul gave him one last spin.

"Turn around three times and catch who you can!" Josh Paul ran and the chase began. Tom lunged for Josh Paul but missed. When Tom started my direction, I jumped to the side, careful not to make a sound. Then I splashed across the creek. Getting wet was more fun than the game.

"What is that on your backside?" Prissy came up behind me. "Is that your bonnet?" She poked at my covering and laughed. "Look, Adele, she has her bonnet around her bumpkin. Maybe she wet her pants."

"Maybe she looked in the mirror and thought it was her face!" Adele laughed and Prissy joined her. Soon everyone was looking at me instead of Tom. No one noticed him at all. He fumbled and then fell all over Prissy, knocking her into the creek. Her dress was soaked and the backside of it was covered in red clay.

"What is that on your backside?" I asked pointing to the back of her pink gingham dress. "It looks like you did more than wet your pants!"

Everyone laughed. Then, when we had all had a chance to get wet, we lost interest in the game. The boys began playing baseball with the men, and the girls started talking about the boys. I wasn't able to do either. One, because I was a girl, and the other because I couldn't talk about my feelings for Josh Paul. My feelings were too strong and deep to share with a bunch of giggling girls. They were the kind you share with your best friend or sister, and I didn't have one anymore.

While we ate Mrs. Bulew's chokecherry pie—she won the blue ribbon for the fifth year in a row—as usual, conversations turned toward fencing and nesters, cattle sales and changes.

Claude Cornhurst stepped up on a wagon bed and spoke as he strutted across its weather-beaten surface. "Changes can be a good thing." He turned to the side where bushes grew and spit. "We slowed the spread of tick fever with barbwire. And them homesteaders, they move on when times get tough. Most of us have been around long enough to know how to handle undesirables. We nudge them on to pasture up with their own breed."

I noticed most of the people in the crowd lowered their eyes and shook their heads as Claude spoke. A few nodded in agreement.

"My point is—" Claude drawled out in his slow corny voice. "It's about time you got to the point, Claude," one of the Tule Ranch cowboys prodded. He was joined by others who heckled and teased Claude. "Make it and get down, Cornhurst, so someone with something to say can get up there."

"Hold your spurs still, boys." Claude waved his hands toward the men. His smooth palms proved his lack of labor as much as his broad belly did. "I just think we need to stop a bad seed before it grows and spreads its thorns."

The crowd grew quiet.

"Now, I like the ladies."

"As often as he can find one blind enough to be seen with him," a cowboy interrupted. Hoots and laughter followed.

"Jack, I don't see no woman standing at your mangy side." Claude took control of the group once more. "This here women's rights malarkey is spreading like wildfire up north, and we just don't want any more of it here." He paused and looked around. "Women need to stay in the kitchen, not horning in on the cattle business. Women don't know nothing about cattle or dickering good deals. They need to be home raising their kids."

Blood rushed to my face when I realized Claude's point was Mama. I watched the others for a reaction. Some shook their heads. Some looked away but most nodded in agreement. Many of those who agreed with Claude were women.

"Are you sure you aren't just afraid of the competition?" Mr. Younger called out.

"Well, it's true that I sell cattle for some of the smaller ranchers." Claude puffed his chest out and walked to the other end of the flat bed. "But I'll bet my best bull that the lady in question couldn't get a better deal.

"Excuse me, Mr. Cornhurst." Hans Schleicher's soft voice

was barely audible above the clapping of the men who agreed.

"Listen," Claude quieted the crowded. "Here's Mr. Schleicher. Let him tell you about the money I made for him." Claude helped Mr. Schleicher up on the wagon beside him.

"It's true, Mr. Cornhurst got for me good prices last autumn." The kind German held his hat in his hands as he spoke.

I felt my temples pound with anger. I couldn't believe the man would sneak out to our dugout asking for Mama's help, and then support Claude in public. His gentleness was a stark comparison to Claude's Banty-rooster ways.

"But Mr. Cornhurst," Mr. Schleicher said, "if it's a new bull we're betting, I could use a new bull." His solemn face broke into a slight smile. "I recently hired Mrs. Jones to represent me for spring cattle sales." Claude leaned over and said something to Mr. Schleicher. But he pulled away from Claude and continued, "Mrs. Jones almost doubled my profits over what I made by selling through you. And she sold the same number of Herefords on futures."

Low whistles and mumbles spread through the crowd. I had learned from Miss Gibson that future sales meant selling cattle you hadn't produced yet. Those that were still babies or hadn't even been born. The men nearby raised an eyebrow and listened more intently to Mr. Schleicher.

"I recommend Mrs. Jones as a cattle agent to anyone, including you, Mr. Cornhurst. And I don't want your best bull." He hopped down with the help of some of the cowboys nearby. Others slapped him on the back or shook his hand.

I glanced over at Mama. She was talking to Mrs. Younger as though she hadn't heard a word spoken from the wagon. Everyone laughed, and then another cowboy told a story of Colonel Charles Goodnight. That was followed by a rehashing of the War Between the States.

Soon the shadows grew long and one by one everyone

headed for their wagons. There was Miss Gibson holding hands with that cowboy. Romantic stuff! Yuck! All I needed was for the best teacher ever to get married and stop teaching. I searched for Mama and the boys. Augusta was playing chess with Mr. Bulew. Jackson was talking Mrs. Bulew's ears off. As I got closer to our picnic basket, I heard Mama.

"Mr. Cornhurst?" Mama's voice came from behind the Younger's wagon.

A deep voice faded into a whisper. I peeked around the corner of the wagon and saw Claude Cornhurst, his head close to Mama's. He was talking softly.

"Yes, I'll be happy to." Mama told him.

"Thank you, ma'am." Claude tipped his hat in her direction and then quickly looked from side to side to see if anyone was watching.

I stared in disbelief. Why would Mama be talking to him? Didn't she hear all the things he had said about her? Besides, he was so dumb even his horse had to tell him how to find the barn. What if Mama was getting sweet on Mr. Cornhurst?

Mama took his hand. I turned away unable to watch anymore. This was terrible. When I turned back to see more, I ran smack into Mama.

"Shyanne, what are you doing?" Her face was lit by a smile.

"What are you doing?" I asked. My upper lip curled of its own free will. "And why were you holding hands with Claude Cornhurst behind the wagon?"

"We were shaking hands."

"He wanted to talk with me in private." She laughed and leaned close. "Mr. Cornhurst has been my biggest opponent at the cattlemen's association." She made her voice sound like Claude's, "Women don't know nothing about cattle or dickering good deals. They need to be home raising kids." Then back in her own voice, she continued, "Claude didn't want anyone to hear when he asked me to sell his herd."

"Sell his cattle herd?" I asked in disbelief—and relief. "He's got quite a few head."

"He sure does," Mama agreed, "and I'll make enough to keep us in groceries through the winter."

I thought about the fees Mama would get from the Cornhurst's cattle sales as we loaded into the Youngers' wagon. Another reunion picnic had ended, and Swisher County was beginning its tenth year.

Chapter Thirteen

August was tolerable only because I knew September's cool crisp nights would soon blow across the plains and school would begin. The fierce summer heat burned all the way to the bone. Lack of rain and grasshoppers bigger than buffalo made the nights longer. Jackson made the days longer. Mama was busy with her cattle sales and feeling poorly. Some days she'd be gone from sun-up to sun-down or pounding the keys of the little typewriter long into the night. The next day she wouldn't get out of bed until seven o'clock, and she'd be back in it by noon.

Near the last of August, I decided to take the big boys down to the creek to fish so Mama could rest. The creek was almost too low for a tadpole to swim, but I helped the boys catch grasshoppers and bait their hooks. After we had been there for about a half hour, Augusta got restless.

"I'm hungry," he said.

Murfrees looked at me with a pitiful expression and echoed, "Me, too."

"We'll head back soon," I answered. Then I looked at Jackson to see how he was doing. He had insisted on fishing up the creek by himself. "Jackson," I called, "you 'bout ready to go?"

"I don't want to go back. I ain't hungry," he yelled. If everyone else had wanted to stay, he would have wanted to go. I sighed with exasperation. "We'll stay for a little while."

As the boys discussed who was going to catch the biggest fish, I looked out across the prairie. Life was changing. I'd be thirteen soon. Josh Paul would be fourteen and he'd have to stay home more and more to help with the crops. He talked of college. Miss Gibson said he needed to go. I dreamed of going with him, but I knew it would never happen. Mama would need me. Suddenly, I didn't want life to change. I didn't even want school to start, because I'd be expected to sit and talk instead of play hoops or climb on the windmill. On the few windless days, the boys took turns spinning the paddles. Last year the girls thought I was a disgrace when I wanted to climb to the top.

When I begged for a turn, Priscilla said, "You just want to show your bloomers off to the boys."

Josh Paul defended me. "Priscilla, I've seen your bloomers many times"—everyone laughed and he added—"hanging on the line behind your house." Then he said, "Shrimp, you better stay on the lower level of the windmill. You're still so little the wind up that high will blow you all the way to the coast."

Everything would change at school this year, maybe even the teacher. That long-legged cowboy had been courting Miss Gibson all summer. If she married, she'd have to quit teaching, and we'd have a new teacher who would think I was stupid like all the others had. Miss Gibson thought I was smart.

No. I didn't want life to change, but I didn't want it to stay the same either.

A smell drew my thoughts away from the coming school year. The western sky had turned from bright blue to a grayish black. I had seen the sky green, which usually meant hail, and deep blue meant rainstorms, but I had never seen the horizon this color of smoky grey. A chill swept over me. Smoke!

"Sweet Jesus, help us!" I gasped.

"I'm telling," Augusta said. "Shyanne is using Jesus' name in the bad way."

"That was a prayer, for sure!" I said as I grabbed the fishing poles and pushed the boys toward the house as quickly as I could move them. "And that is a prairie fire. Big, wide and moving fast."

"Where?" Augusta stopped and searched the prairie. Jackson protested my push and joined his brother.

"I don't see no fire," he muttered. Murfrees just put his hands on his hips and stood by his brother like he knew what he was doing. I grabbed him and yelled at Augusta and Jackson. "You stand and watch if you want. That black sky is coming this way! Every blade of prairie grass between here and it will be ablaze before we can get Mama and the babies to safety." I started running toward the house, knowing they would be close behind.

"Mama, fire!" I screamed when I was close enough for her to hear. "Mama!"

She had the door open and ran out to meet us. "It looks like a bad one," she warned as she headed for the barn. "Help me with the wagon, Shyanne. Jackson, get everything you can carry out of the house." She spoke fast, but her voice remained calm and controlled. "We'll have to try to get away from it."

I knew better. There was no way to outrun a prairie fire. Last fall, ten-year-old Clay Willingham burned in his cabin with his ma and pa working in the field not half a mile away. They couldn't get to him. People had two chances in a fire like the one that loomed on the horizon before us: you wet everything down, and you pray the fire will turn or burn itself out.

Mama reached the barn and pulled the tarp back off the wagon. "Augusta, catch the chickens and put them in a sack," she ordered. "Jackson pick up anything you can and set it out on the porch. Murfrees, help Mama and watch the babies."

Murfrees smiled and ran into the house, excited to help. Mama pushed on the wagon, but it wouldn't budge. Her face distorted in pain and she grabbed her stomach. She had gotten so big with this new baby, I knew it would either be another set of twins or it would come before September.

"Mama, don't!" I said. "Let me help." I pushed and still it wouldn't move. We hitched up Sally. I scraped the dirt from around the wheels and we rocked it. Finally, it moved. The smoke burned my nose and minutes later my eyes began to sting.

"Hurry!" Mama warned as we threw everything on the wagon. I picked up Russell and Shawnee, placing them under the seat with the tarp over them. Then Mama grabbed pictures, food, water and a small bundle and headed toward the wagon. I emptied the water barrel on the sod roof of our house, hoping it would keep the fire from burning the support-beams. Then I jumped in beside my brothers.

"Let's go!" she yelled. She tried to climb in the wagon. The baby in her tummy made it difficult, so I took her hand and tugged as hard as I could. She got in as the tongues of yellow and red flames lapped up the grass between our house and town. I thought about Miss Gibson, the school, Bulew's Store and even Prissy. Would anything be left?

We drove to the creek as fast as Sally could take us, racing jackrabbits, antelope, coyotes and a menagerie of reptiles. By the time we rolled the wagon into the creek, the fire was sweeping our roof top, devouring everything in its path.

Mama tossed the canvas tarp into the muddy creek and then she and I spread it over the wagon. "Get in the wagon, Shyanne," she called.

Sally, wide-eyed and skittish, jumped and bolted. It took all I could do to hold her.

"I better hold her head," I yelled back. Mama came around the wagon.

"We have to let her go," she said unhitching the cow. Sally was one of the family. I couldn't believe Mama was sending her out to be barbecued.

"I can hold her, Mama."

"Get in the wagon, now!" she ordered harshly and grabbed my arm. Then she held me close. "Don't fret. Sally will be safer on her own. Animals have a special knowledge. Now, hurry!"

"I better help you in first." Even in the fear that blazed

around us, I chuckled. "I think it'll be easier to push than pull on you."

Mama laughed, too. As she stepped up, I noticed her face grimace in pain again.

Heat waves rippled between our dugout and the creek like a distorted looking-glass, twisting our home out of shape. Suddenly, I felt a great longing for it to be spared. I had hated its dirt floors, cramped room and sod walls full of spiders and salamanders. Not having it would be much worse. I knew it meant we would have to leave. Leave Tulia, leave Texas and leave Josh Paul. The fire spread up the creek bed toward his house, and I gave up fighting my tears.

Heat and smoke engulfed us. Shawnee began to wheeze, and Russell was coughing. Mama had dipped cloths in the creek and gave them to us to tie around our faces. I couldn't stand it over my eyes. I felt like if I could see the fire, it couldn't reach out and grab us.

Under the tarp, Murfrees and Russell cuddled as close to Mama as possible. Augusta sat at her knees with Shawnee in his lap. I felt Jackson inch up next to me, shivering and sweating at the same time. He hadn't had much to do with me since Shenandoah died. I couldn't decide if he somehow knew I had hurt her or if he was afraid to love me for fear I'd go away too. I ruffled his hair and kissed his dirty cheek as I pulled the wet cloth over his face and cradled him in my lap.

Mama surprised me by singing—not one of those slow, dreary songs. Old people sang songs like, "It Is Better Farther On" or "Amazing Grace" when there's trouble. Mama sang "Halley, Hallelujah," one of the songs all the young people liked and all the old folks thought was sinful. I loved it.

The Devil's dead and I am glad,
Oh Halley, Hallelujah!
The Devil's dead and I am glad,

Oh Halley, Hallelujah!

The Devil's dead and gone to hell
Oh Halley, Hallelujah!
I hope he's there for quite a spell
Oh Halley, Hallelujah!

Shout! Shout! We're gaining ground
Oh Halley, Hallelujah!
The love of God is coming down
Oh Halley, Hallelujah!"

Mama sang as Augusta and Murfrees shouted on the "Hally, Hallelujah!" As I joined in on the last verse, so did Jackson.

My uncle had an old red hound
Oh Hally, Hallelujah!
He chased the rabbits round and round
Oh Hally, Hallelujah!"

Long after the fire burned away and we removed our kerchiefs, we stayed in the wagon until the embers cooled. We sang the quiet, old songs that now felt comforting instead of boring. Mama opened a tin bucket and gave us each a biscuit. Her voice grew weak and, in the dim light, I could see her face pale.

The boys fell asleep. I slept, too. Sometime later, a muffled groan—much like a wild animal caught in a trap—woke me. Mama had a pillow over her face and rocked back and forth.

I slid Jackson from my lap and crawled to touch Mama. She jerked her head up. There was a frenzied look in her eyes, but she quickly hid it with a smile and clutched my hand. "You're going to have to help me, Shyanne," she whispered. "The baby is coming."

"Help you! Me?" I asked. I had slipped into the room

when the granny woman came to deliver Russell, but I couldn't help deliver a baby. I was terrified. Besides, I hadn't been able to help my sister. "I can't, Mama! I don't know how."

"I do most of it by myself." She paused and breathed like a puppy that had been chasing the big dogs. "You have to know, in case I pass out."

Pass out—the words swam around in my head and taunted me. She could die. I had never thought of Mama dying. I grabbed her hand and squeezed it as if I could stop the birth. Mama pointed to the last bundle she had packed in the wagon.

"In that cloth, you'll find everything we need for the delivery," Mama said. "After the baby comes tie a string around the cord and cut it."

I unrolled the bundle like it was a snake coiled, waiting to strike.

Mama winced in pain, then gasped as she gave orders. "Lay the blanket here at my feet."

I quickly tried to do as she directed, but my hands shook and I dropped everything.

"Mama, I'm so scared," I cried. Scooping up the bundle, I dropped it again.

She smoothed her hair back and opened her eyes wide, intent on staying alert. Then she spoke, "I'm not afraid. There's not a person in the world I trust more than you." She groaned slightly. "You're my best friend, the woman I trust the most."

Mama's words were wonderful, but they didn't make me any smarter about birth. Her stomach felt hard as I brushed against it. The movement was terrifying, but she trusted me. I swiped at the tears on my face and took a deep breath. "I'll try, Mama."

"I know you will," she whispered.

As I followed her orders, my hands seemed as though they belonged to someone else. I laid out the string and the knife, washed my hands in whiskey, and prayed each time she shut her eyes and pushed against the side of the wagon. When Mama stopped giving me directions, I held her hand and washed her face, just as I had seen the granny do. I gave her a stick to chew on and offered her water. All that I had seen others do for her in the past, I did.

Nothing had prepared me for the wonderful joy of the baby's birth. It happened quickly. One minute, Mama pushed her feet against the wagon sideboard, and the next moment a squirming, red-faced baby lay in my hands.

"It's beautiful," I cried.

"Give it a swat on the backside," Mama ordered through gasping breaths.

I patted its little bare-bottom, but nothing happened. My heart skipped a beat. When the granny woman had swatted Murfrees, he had let out such a wail that it woke the neighbors.

"Again, Shiloh," Mama demanded. "Harder!"

The baby's skin looked blue. Fear quivered through me like distant thunder. I slapped the baby once more. It gasped and then after a moment that seemed a lifetime, it cried.

"Thank God!" Mama said as she leaned back, happy tears glistening on her checks. "Lay the baby on the blanket."

Carefully, I laid the baby on its side.

"Now, wrap the string around and around the cord going to its belly." Mama's voice spoke the words and my hands acted, as if she directed their movements. "Tie a hard knot—yes, there, around the cord," Mama directed as she struggled to sit upright.

I followed her directions.

"Now, cut the cord about as long as your hand, and wrap the baby in the blanket," she said.

My hand trembled as I picked up the knife. The cord didn't look like part of the baby or part of Mama, but it was flesh, and I didn't know if I could do it.

"One quick stroke," Mama encouraged with a matter of fact voice. "Just like cutting hair. It won't hurt either of us."

Quickly, I did as she said. Then, I wrapped the blanket around the baby and handed the little bundle to Mama.

Mama winced a little as she turned to take it. Then she smiled through tears that Shenandoah would have called heavenly dew-drops. "Thank you, honey." She pulled the blanket back and looked at the baby more closely.

The baby's cry woke Jackson. He was at my elbow, half-awake and very surprised. "What's that?" he asked.

"It's a . . ." Mama paused. A frown crossed her brow. "This isn't our usual Jones' order." Mama handed the baby back to me. "Here, Shyanne, hold your little sister, while I finish cleaning up."

"A girl!" Jackson groaned.

"Sister?" I tried to swallow the lump wedged in my throat.

"A sister!" Mama held her out to me.

I couldn't take her. I didn't deserve her.

"Take her," Mama ordered.

I slipped my hand under the baby's tiny head and wrapped the blanket around her tightly. She stopped crying and blinked up at me with big eyes that had a promise of blue around their dark centers. Her tiny hand wrapped around my finger. "You're my only little sister," I cooed softly. "I love you and you don't even know it."

"Yes she does," Mama said as she rolled the blanket up and laid back on the pillow. "A sister's love is like God's grace. You don't have to be good enough. Sisters always know you love them. Even when you're angry and say hurtful words, they know. They know you love them."

Mama's words lifted the heavy burden I had carried since February. Shenandoah knew. She knew I loved her.

"What will you name her?" I asked and waited for Mama's answer.

"You helped with her birth," Mama closed her eyes. "What will you name her?"

117

"Me?"

"Yes, you. I'm all out of names," she answered in a sleepy voice. "We named the others after the place they were born. But, no child should be named Tule Creek."

"Let's name her tadpole!" Jackson suggested.

"Shiloh will name her." Mama closed her eyes to rest.

"I'm calling her Tadpole." Jackson ran to wake up his brothers.

"I can't think of a name," I mumbled. "I don't know anything pretty enough."

"It'll come to you," Mama said. "Don't make her wait too long.

Chapter Fourteen

Four days later, the amazing wonder of the birth lingered over me as we cleaned the dugout. It was schorched but standing. We found Sally but the lean-to was burned beyond repair. Our two heifers were scattered or dead.

The sun stretched its long orange and pink fingers across the charred prairie. The boys fed the few chickens we had saved. Mama rocked the baby and life continued, in spite of the fire and Papa's absence.

I left the dugout early the next morning with Josh Paul and his father. We needed supplies. The Younger place had escaped the blaze, so Mr. Younger promised to help Miss Gibson get the schoolhouse repaired. He replaced the windmill frame that burned in the fire. Josh Paul and I cleaned the windows.

"Pa was telling me that the windmill saved the school," Josh Paul talked as we worked. "When it fell during the fire, the tank on top splashed gallons of water on the ground. It's a good thing the school didn't burn."

I nodded. "Last year, I would have loved for the school to burn," I said, scrubbing black soot off the windows. "I hated school. Now, I almost like it." The barrel I stood on wobbled as I jumped to the ground.

Josh Paul laughed suddenly.

"What's funny?" I watched him carefully to see if he was laughing at me.

"You are!" He swiped a sooty rag on my nose.

Pushing his hand away, I added, "Now that I have black on my face, I guess I am." I tried to focus on the tip of my nose to see if I could rub it off.

"No." He looked into my eyes like a friend who sees past all the pretending and into your heart. "You're starting to act grown up, like those girls who sit at picnic celebrations and never play any of the games."

"I am not!" I argued, knowing the cow-chip toss had already lost its allure. "Look what growing up has done to Miss Gibson," I said. "She's getting all moony over that cowboy. She'll probably be quitting to get married."

"No, she told my ma she'd teach at least one more year," Josh Paul said. "Seems they're planning a wedding next July."

"Well, at least we have next year," I sighed.

"Yoo hoo!" Priscilla's shrill voice pierced our conversation. "Josh Paul, I hoped I'd find you here." Dressed like a little princess, she smiled at Josh Paul. Then she and Adele looked at me as if I were one of the rags I had used to clean the smoke from the schoolhouse windows.

"I can't tell what my basket for next week's social will look like." Prissy acted shy and sweet like a spider asking a fly into its web. "I will say, my basket's bow will be the shade of this dress." She flipped her pink skirt and giggled.

"Now, you'll know which one to bid on," Adele said, gushing laughter that sounded like a pig rooting in a turnip patch.

"Is that right?" Josh Paul answered. "That's too bad, because I hate pink." Priscilla's face dropped.

"Well, what is your favorite color?" she asked, her lips drawn together in a pout.

Josh Paul looked at me and grinned. "Whatever color Shyanne's box is." Then he took my hand, right in front of Prissy and Adele. They left in a huff.

We stood there for a moment, both of us a little shy at the new feelings in our friendship. Suddenly, he dropped my hand and began clearing the scorched weeds from around the building. He pulled his miracle tree up from its place by the door. It was

120

parched and dead.

"I'm sorry about the tree," I said softly.

"You knew all along I had planted it," he said. "My uncle brought it back from the mountains."

"Yes. But it made me feel good to know you went to all that trouble to make me think a miracle could happen."

"It didn't work." He plucked off a handful of needles and let them drop between his fingers.

"No. It was better," I said. "It proved that you're my friend and you care about me." Kneeling next to him, I started pulling weeds. "I've been thinking about the snow, the fire and life." I sat back in the shade and leaned against the building. Looking out across the countryside distorted by the heat waves, I realized I had been seeing things out of focus. Since the baby was born, life seemed like the ground after it's been burned—clear, ready for a fresh start. "Maybe I am wrong about things never working out for the good. I've been wrong about a lot of things lately."

Josh Paul's mouth dropped open in disbelief. I commented before he could.

"I've been spreading gloom thicker than chickens spread you-know-what," I said. "I know! Admitting I'm wrong isn't like me."

"Does this mean you believe in happy-ever-after?" he asked.

Biting on my lip, I thought before I answered. "Yes, there's happy-ever-after. There's a power in believing in people and hoping for the best." I was unsure of how to explain it to Josh Paul without his laughing at me. I picked my words cautiously. "But, happy and ever-after don't come at the same time. There are a few bad times sprinkled in with the good ones." Turning the barrel over, I tossed a handful of weeds into it. "I've been spending too much time thinking about the bad times."

The air between us sparked. Josh Paul went back to his

work, pulling the trash and weeds from around the schoolhouse. Moments later, he asked, "What did you name the baby?"

"Nothing yet. I'm hoping, I'll think of a name pretty enough."

"She's a pretty one, that's for sure."

"Hope," I whispered. "That's it!" Then I added with excitement, "I'll call my baby sister Hope."

"Hope? It's strange for someone who spreads gloom thicker than you-know-what to choose a name like Hope." He leaned close to me. "But then, you're a strange girl, Shiloh Anne." His smile made my stomach flip. Then he kissed my cheek.

I felt the blood rush to my face and turned away to avoid his eyes. Something sharp poked my back. "Ouch!" I yelped.

As I moved over, I saw the ragged stump of Miss Gibson's tree covered over in dead grass. Josh Paul pulled the weeds away from the stump reverently.

My fingers cleared the rubble from the opposite side. The dirt felt warm beneath my fingers—the memories of the tree warm in my mind. It had been the perfect Christmas tree. The joy on Shenandoah's face filled my heart with memories.

A speck of light green appeared in the dirt. I brushed the soil away, revealing a tender shoot growing from the stump of the little pine tree. It uncurled in my hand and stretched toward the sun.

As I touched the soft needles, I realized that miracles are not only great events that rarely happen, but small events that happen everyday—the birth of a baby, a damaged root pushing through hard soil to form a tender shoot, and surviving the coldest day in Texas.

"It's a miracle!" I whispered.

"It sure enough is!" he answered in a voice deep with emotion.

"It needs water," Josh Paul said as he sprang up and ran

to the windmill.

I looked at the new frame and the paddles Mr. Younger had just repaired. The blades stood motionless in the bright sky.

"You're going to have to turn the wheel to get water," I reminded him. "There's not a breath of wind."

Josh Paul looked up at the windmill paddles and then looked at me. With a slight grin he challenged me. "I'll race you to the top!"

ABOUT THE AUTHOR

Growing up in the Texas Panhandle, Peggy Purser Freeman was fascinated by stories of the pioneer spirit that carved homes out of the wilderness. She hopes to keep that spirit alive through her writing.

A resident of Cedar Hill, Texas, Ms. Freeman has worked in the Texas school system for twenty years and is currently computer technology manager for the Arlington Independent School District. She enjoys fishing, camping and researching historical sites with her family.